The Rift Chronicles

Book One – Micah One

By
R. A. Harolds

Table of Contents

Prologue-Micah

Still dripping soap and shame, Micah had trudged through the gates with all the dignity of a damp ferret. Behind him, a janitor angrily shouted about "sentient bubbles in the ventilation again."

His official record read:

MICAH, Apprentice. Expelled for:

1) Reckless enchantment of cleaning supplies,

2) Gross misuse of soap-based conjuration, and

3) Releasing a mop with romantic feelings for brooms.

What it didn't mention was the "raining frogs incident."

It had started with an innocent attempt at atmospheric magic. Micah had been aiming for a dramatic cloud effect during Presentation Week. A light drizzle. A little thunder. Something that said, *I'm competent but whimsical.*

What he got was frogs.

Thousands of them.

For three hours.

It rained frogs in every hallway, library, and soup bowl. The headmaster slipped on one. A senior enchantment student tried to duel a particularly muscular toad. *Chaos.*

Micah claimed it was "meteorologically educational."

No one laughed.

And then came the slugs.

That one wasn't even intentional. He'd been practicing a transmutation charm meant to conjure clean socks. Instead, it delivered precisely 137 garden slugs directly into the dormitory beds.

They were slimy. They were fast. And they were loud for reasons no one could explain.

"I don't even know where they came from," Micah had said helplessly as students shrieked and flung bedcovers into the courtyard.

The next day, his dorm room door had been sealed shut with three different sigils, a sock nailed to it like a warning flag.

And then came the pants-melting incident, the mop uprising, and the brief possession of the breakfast buffet (don't ask).

By the time the Conclave gathered to review his fate, Micah was already halfway through packing. His roommate was still finding slugs in his pillowcase.

"You're not untalented," the headmaster had said with a tired groan, "just... profoundly unlucky."

Micah had nodded solemnly, clutching his spellbook and a damp bag of emergency scones.

No graduation robes. No formal wand license. No farewell cake. Just a sponge, a scroll, and a reputation that would follow him like a ripple in the ocean.

Chapter One: Embers in the Dark

The room stank of burned thyme, old secrets, and something unmistakably… swampy.

Dozens of flickering candles guttered in high alcoves, casting wild shadows across cracked stone and weathered tomes. Jars of unidentifiable things—some of them still twitching—lined the shelves like grim trophies. At the center stood a long, scorched alchemy table, and behind it, hunched and scowling, the wizard stirred a cauldron with a spoon that may once have been silver. Emphasis on once.

He muttered under his breath, one gnarled finger trailing down the pages of a thick, leather-bound grimoire.

"Vorthenith… akar'ael… sibiluth…," he growled. The final syllable caught on his tongue like a splinter.

There was a pop. Then, a crack.

Then—

BOOM.

One of the containers near the edge of the table exploded, scattering jagged glass across the room. A trail of purple steam hissed toward the ceiling as the wizard flung the spellbook across the room, where it struck a stack of cursed skulls and sent them tumbling like very disappointed bowling pins.

"Blasted, botched, brainless scribes!" he snarled, storming over to retrieve the book. His hands trembled not with fear, but fury — focused, simmering, and centuries old.

At the bottom of the incantation page, the ink was smudged with what looked suspiciously like dried honey. Or possibly toad bile. Either way, the final component of the spell was illegible.

"I must need another ingredient," he muttered, "or someone misspelled Tormik's ether again. Idiots."

He slammed the book shut and collapsed onto the bench, long fingers drumming the stone table with a sharp, impatient rhythm. Sparks from the cauldron fizzled beside him, ignored.

Then—a knock.

Not the hesitant knock of a servant. Not the booming authority of a mage. This was the awkward, reluctant knock of someone caught between a sense of duty and a fear of being incinerated.

The wizard sighed heavily. "By the Third Circle's cracked chalice," he muttered, standing.

He yanked the door open to reveal a pale, panting messenger in the livery of his estate — mud-splattered and clutching a satchel with trembling hands.

"I'm sorry to interrupt, sir," the young man said quickly, ducking his head, "but there's been… a development. Regarding a past indiscretion."

The wizard's eyes narrowed until they were slits of molten iron. "I told you never to mention that situation again."

The courier swallowed hard but didn't back down.

"Yes, sir. You did, sir. Very clearly. But a rider came from the Academy with a sealed message. About the outcome of—er—that incident. The one involving the child."

For a moment, the only sound was the bubbling of the disgruntled cauldron behind him.

The wizard stepped back into the room, motioning sharply, "Inside. Ten minutes."

The messenger followed cautiously, as one might follow a cornered bear with an overdue tax bill.

"He insisted on speaking to you in person," the man added quickly. "We avoided the guards - I used the tunnels. Very discreet."

The wizard's voice was barely a whisper now, but it scraped like sandpaper.

"I care nothing for—yes, I will say it, the babe I left on their doorstep. That was resolved years ago. I told them to destroy the records. I warned them."

"Yes, sir. They must have…misplaced the warning."

The wizard stared down into the ruined potion, his reflection rippling like a forgotten ghost.

"You will bring this rider to me. He will say his piece, and then you will see him to his horse and out of my sight. Do you understand?"

"Perfectly, sir," the messenger said, bowing with visible relief.

He turned to go. Behind him, the wizard murmured under his breath. Not a spell. A name. A name he hadn't spoken in nearly two decades. *Micah*...

The candlelight flickered. And somewhere in the ruins of memory, the past began to stir.

Chapter Two: The Boy, the Menace, the Mistake

The rider stood in the flickering gloom of the alchemist's hall, his boots dripping onto the rune-etched floor. His traveling cloak was soaked with rain, and a damp strand of hair clung awkwardly to his forehead as he bowed low before the wizard.

He didn't appear to be a man who enjoyed confrontation. Then again, Erius had drawn the short straw. And when the short straw meant delivering news to the most volatile wizard this side of the Blood Coast, well… that was just his luck.

The wizard, still smoldering from his earlier explosion — literal and otherwise — loomed by the hearth, arms crossed, brow furrowed deep enough to trap spells in.

"Speak. And be precise."

Erius cleared his throat. "As you know, sir…" he began, choosing his words as carefully as one might defuse a magical landmine, "…the young charge you left in our care—on the Academy's doorstep, to be specific—in his earliest hours, has… grown."

The wizard did not blink. Erius took this as permission to continue.

"He is now of age. And his aptitude for magic, while… considerable, is unpredictable at best. At worst…" He hesitated, "Well, we've had casualties of confidence. Some minor injuries. The occasional property loss. And one frog incident that turned into an ecological dilemma."

The wizard's glare did not soften.

"Out with it."

Erius straightened, voice steadying. "We expelled him, sir."

The silence that followed was so heavy it pressed against the walls. The wizard's eye twitched. "You what?"

"We had no choice," Erius said quickly, "he miscasts more often than he breathes. In his first year, he set fire to the moat. We don't even know how. He once tried to summon a study familiar and accidentally called forth a mildly aggressive goose that haunted the grounds for months. And last week…"

He swallowed.

"…he tried to clean his robes with a minor transmutation and nearly collapsed the north wing."

The wizard's voice dropped, low and cold as glacial stone. "You let him out into the world… knowing his magic is unstable?"

Erius took a cautious step back. "He's of age. And the tuition rules are clear. When a student comes of age, we are permitted to continue or end instruction. We endured a great many years of chaos, sir. But the faculty voted unanimously. He's out."

The wizard's fingers twitched at his sides, sparks dancing between them like impatient lightning.

"And what would you have me do, then? Hunt him through the kingdoms like a runaway curse? Retrieve him, scrape his mistakes off the village walls, and put him back in your precious school?!"

"We would prefer," Erius said carefully, "that you leave him where he is. We are no longer responsible for him. He is a free agent… a menace, yes, but no longer our problem. His flirty disposition and his ineptitude with spellwork have made him both admired and feared by the wrong sorts of people."

The wizard turned, pacing in tight, stormy circles. His voice dropped to a venomous murmur. "I warned your kind. When I handed him over, I said there was power in his blood. And you cast him out like a failed experiment."

"You left him with us," Erius snapped, finally showing a flicker of backbone. "You washed your hands of him and left no name, no history. What else were we supposed to do?"

The wizard turned on him like a striking snake.

"You were supposed to control him. Now he is out there, wandering, curious, unstable, untaught, and unleashed."

He jabbed a finger toward the door.

"Go. Return to your gilded tower and your cowed masters. If he unleashes something he can't stop, the consequences are yours. I will find him myself."

Erius bowed stiffly, retreating toward the exit with all the dignity he could muster.

"And do not return here," the wizard added darkly, "next time, I won't be in a listening mood."

The door slammed behind the rider, echoing down the corridor like a final word. The wizard stood alone in the chamber, the fire at his back casting long, jagged shadows across the stone. He stared into the cauldron once more—at the potion that had fizzled, sputtered, and failed. Just like him. He didn't say the name aloud. But it hung in the air anyway.

Micah.

Chapter Three: The Spell that should not be cast

The wizard stood in silence long after the rider had gone, the embers of the hearth cracking softly in the silence. He didn't move. Didn't blink. His mind spiraled in slow, venomous circles. He had left Micah with the Academy for a reason. They had the wards, the rituals, the endless manuals and instructors, and boring, structured days to bleed the wildness out of him. To grind down the edges. To blunt the power. But they had failed. Now he would have to pick up the pieces. He hated loose ends, especially when those ends could level a village while trying to conjure a mop.

He turned slowly, his long robes whispering against the stone as he moved deeper into the chamber, past the alchemy table, beyond the summoning circle burned into the floor, and down a stairwell that hadn't been touched in years.

The torches here were different. They didn't burn with fire. They burned with memory. As he passed, each one flared to life with a hiss, glowing blue, then violet, then deep, furious red. The final door was made of old obsidian, veined with runes that pulsed when they recognized him. The sigil in the center flared at the press of his hand.

"I swore I'd never open this door again," he muttered.

But promises were made in optimism. And broken in necessity. With a groan of ancient stone, the door opened.

The Chamber of Binding

The room beyond was cold and dry — freezing in the way time is cold, and dry in the way bones are dry. The walls were adorned with symbols from a long-forgotten language. In the center: a pedestal. On the pedestal, a book. No title. No clasp.

It was bound in old leather, with a spine that twitched faintly at his approach. He took a breath, long and sharp, and opened it.

The pages whispered.

They knew him.

The spell he sought was buried halfway through, between a map of the nine shattered planes and a diagram of a mind unraveling in script.

He ran a finger down the page.

Paused.

"No shortcuts this time," he murmured.

This magic wasn't meant for searching. It was meant for hunting.

The spell begins

He began to chant—low and rhythmic, a voice like oil poured over ancient steel. The shadows twisted around him. The torches dimmed. The walls pulsed. And one by one, the runes on the floor lit up, circling him in crimson light. From the cauldron at the center of the room, the brew hissed. Not green now. Not foul. But bright white—and burning hot. His hands moved in practiced motions, conjuring symbols midair that shimmered and bled as they hung above the book.

The spell would find Micah.

Wherever he went.

Whatever magic tried to cloak him.

This was blood calling to blood.

And no magic in the world was older than that.

And then... something strange

As the spell reached its peak, the cauldron erupted with light.

The room shook.

The tower groaned.

And then—

A vision.

Not conjured.

Given.

He saw the boy—not a boy now—but a young man, laughing in the middle of a forest trail, a crooked staff in one hand and sparks flying from his other palm. Around him were strangers—odd ones—a gnome, a minotaur, a bard, and…

A witch.

They looked ridiculous.

But they looked like…

A party.

The wizard reeled back.

The vision snapped.

And the room went still.

"So," he growled, voice low.

"He's not alone."

He closed the book. His eyes glowed faintly with the magic still running through him. And in the silence of the tower, the wizard smiled. But it was not a kind smile.

Chapter Four: Rattling Chains and Rattled Consciences

The cell was everything a dwarf should hate — cramped, clammy, and cut from stone so badly chiseled it looked like the mountain had sneezed, and someone called it architecture.

The walls dripped with the slow, stubborn sweat of centuries. A single iron door was bolted shut with dwarven-made chain — thick, black, and unbreakable. Of course, it was.

Inside sat one miserable occupant, huddled on a pallet covered with what could barely qualify as fabric, smelling faintly of mildew and betrayal. Beside him, a dented tin bucket that had long since declared war on the concept of hygiene.

"Of course," the dwarf muttered, eyeing the lock with a sneer, "it had to be dwarven-forged. I'd have picked any human-made rubbish open in minutes. But no, this one's practically smirking at me."

He kicked the wall half-heartedly and immediately regretted it. He rubbed his sore toe and slumped back with a sigh that had traveled a long road of disappointment to get here.

"This is what I get," he continued under his breath, "for going after the whole purse. Had enough coin for the night. The tavern crowd was generous—even the bearded one tipped well. Should've taken that and gone on my merry, semi-honest way. But nooo. I saw the gleam of a coin I didn't need and got greedy. A bard, they said. A wanderer, they said. I should've stayed on the bloody mountain. At least the goats didn't lock you up for bad decisions."

He let out a groan and stared up at the cracked ceiling, listening to the distant clatter of armor above. Voices drifted down the corridor—low, curt exchanges between guards, then the familiar rattle of keys, the scrape of bolt and hinge, and the groan of doors too old to care. Footsteps. Coming closer. He turned his head toward the corridor beyond his bars.

"Private visit, huh?" he muttered.

"Fancy. Let me guess. A noble's brat wants to see how the poor live. Or maybe the guards got bored and brought me an audience. I'll sing them a dirge with my bucket."

He snorted and leaned back, trying to look as uninterested as possible. But the footsteps stopped. Right at his cell. A throat cleared. He turned.

"You've got the wrong cell," he grumbled, not bothering to rise.

"Go away. I don't know you."

A voice slipped through the shadows like a blade dipped in honey. "But you do."

The dwarf sat up straighter. The speaker stepped closer, just beyond the reach of the dim torchlight.

"Or has your memory shrunk to the size of the coin purses you keep failing to steal?"

There was a sound—clink-chink—the unmistakable rattle of coins in a pouch. Then the voice chuckled. "Does this ring any bells, little dwarf?"

The bard's face tightened.

"You…"

His voice came out rougher than he intended. He recognized that laugh now. That low, lazy, dangerous laugh that curled around a threat like smoke around a blade. This wasn't just any man he'd tried to pickpocket. This was the sort of man whose pouch didn't jingle — it warned.

Chapter Five: The Offer

"I know you, Galdon."

The voice curled through the bars like smoke—low, knowing, and sharp as a dagger in the dark.

"You're a self-proclaimed bard… and a consistently unsuccessful thief."

Galdon didn't flinch. He sat with his back against the cold stone wall, legs casually stretched in front of him. One boot was missing, and the smell in the cell was beginning to reach philosophical levels of bad. He let out a sigh and raised an eyebrow.

Smirking at the shadowed man, Galdon quipped, "I know who I am, you twit. If you're here to monologue me into the grave, just get on with it. As you can see," he gestured broadly to the dank, empty cell, "I'm swamped."

The visitor stepped closer, the light of his torch spilling across the cell bars. It flickered over thick, arched brows pulled low in irritation and a face like a storm-worn cliff—deep lines etched into skin that had seen too many disappointments and possibly caused most of them. As the firelight hit his face, Galdon's stomach dropped. It was him. The old man from the tavern. The one with the fancy coin purse and the annoyingly perceptive eyes. The one Galdon had almost stolen from before a misplaced lute chord and an enormous security goose had ruined everything. Galdon groaned. "You've got to be joking."

"So, you remember me," the man's voice was calm. Too calm. The kind of calm that suggested he'd set fire to villages and written poems about it afterward. "You should be more polite to someone who can get you out of here, little dwarf."

"Little?" Galdon scoffed, crossing his arms, "says the man built like a twig and twice as brittle."

The man didn't smile.

"Taunt me all you want," Galdon added, voice rising a notch. "What's the game? Come to gloat? Should I have chosen a richer target? Laugh at the pathetic bard who thought he could outwit a wizard?"

He spat the word.

The man raised an eyebrow.

"You're not that far gone, then. Yes, Bard. A wizard."

Galdon slumped back and rubbed his eyes.

"Oh, brilliant. I try to pinch one purse, one, and it belongs to the local doomcaster with a penchant for dramatic lighting and dungeon decor. Do all of you rehearse these entrances?"

The wizard leaned slightly closer to the bars, and the flame in his torch flared.

"Make your jokes, dwarf. But I'm not here for revenge. I'm here to make you an offer."

Galdon raised both eyebrows this time. The wizard smiled, but it didn't reach his eyes. "It's an excellent offer. And I'm sure you'll find it irresistible since the alternative is rotting in this cell for five years."

Galdon blinked. "Five?"

The wizard gave a lazy shrug. "It's the standard sentence for attempting to rob a wizard. Six if you succeed. I pulled some strings to keep it on the shorter end."

"Oh, well, thank you for your mercy," Galdon said with acid.

He stood now, arms outstretched, pacing the length of the cell like a performer on stage. "So what is it then? You need a bard to sing your praises while you conjure rain and impress party guests? Maybe you need someone to distract a dragon while you make off with its hoard?"

The wizard leaned forward, eyes narrowing.

"You wouldn't be offering this to just anyone. So why me?"

"Because," the wizard said, voice now as soft as a falling dagger, "you're talented. And too stupid to say No."

The wizard paused. "Someone who knows how to vanish. Someone who can sneak into places others avoid. Someone with no attachments… and no expectations of survival."

Galdon froze mid-step. "Well, that's ominous."

The wizard smirked.

Galdon grinned, and ready to tell the wizard to stuff it, he surprised himself completely by saying, "You know what? You might just be right."

Chapter Six: Terms and Conditions

The wizard's eyes glinted like flint struck in shadow. He took a slow step closer to the bars, and this time, the fire in his torch hissed in sympathy.

"I have a task that needs doing. A quest, if that term makes your bardic heart feel more important."

Galdon didn't flinch, but his jaw tightened.

"You and a few others—handpicked—will complete this task for me. Only when you accept will I tell you the full details. What I will say now is this: it must be done precisely as I outline, and with the companions I've already selected. There will be no substitutions, no bargaining."

He let that sit, heavy and cold.

"It won't be easy."

Galdon's arms crossed. "Is it ever?"

"But should you succeed," the wizard continued, his voice now smooth as silk laced with iron, "you'll earn more than freedom. Your criminal record will be expunged. Wiped away like dust from a scroll. And in addition," he paused, with just enough drama to make Galdon want to slap him, "a sack of gold. Enough to buy your way out of whatever miserable tavern gig you stumble into next."

Galdon stared at him.

Long and hard.

Then slowly, he snarled.

"Quite the choice, wizard. Rot in a cell with my dignity or serve you like some glorified errand boy."

He stepped forward until his nose nearly touched the bars, eyes blazing.

"Fine. I'll take the task. But if you betray me…"

"Stop," the wizard's voice cut through the dungeon like a sword through silk. It wasn't loud. But it echoed. "You are in no position to make threats."

He took another step forward, his presence suddenly massive, like gravity had doubled in the room.

"But I will promise you this: complete the task, and you will get exactly what you deserve."

There was something in his tone. Not menace, finality. Something ancient. Something old and vast crouched behind his words like a beast behind a curtain. Galdon swallowed. It made a sound he hadn't meant anyone to hear.

The wizard turned to the guards.

"Open this cell."

The lead guard stiffened. "Are you certain, Grandmaster? He could be dangerous. He was singing while relieving himself in the bucket. My ears are still recovering."

Galdon raised a brow and grinned. "It's called multitasking."

The wizard didn't even blink. He simply looked at the guard with the sort of expression that made hellhounds whimper and archmages reconsider their hobbies.

"Open. The. Cell."

The guard paled visibly and fumbled with the keys as if they might bite him. With a reluctant clack, the door swung open. Galdon stepped forward, stiff from disuse, but every inch of him radiating defiance. He paused beside the wizard.

"Lead the way, oh mighty task-giver."

"Follow me," the Grandmaster said without looking back.

And, in a rare moment of uncharacteristic wisdom, Galdon followed. He didn't speak. Not yet.

The dungeon corridors stretched out ahead of them—cold, damp, and just as miserable as the cell he'd left behind. The torchlight cast eerie shadows that moved like thoughts in dark corners.

He rubbed his wrists where the shackles had left their mark. He was out of the cell. But he didn't feel free. Not yet. And something told him this so-called task would demand far more than just his hands.

Chapter Seven: Heat, Humility, and the Grimy Mug

By the time they reached the surface, the sun hung low in the sky, a molten disk casting gold fire across the rooftops of the city. The air still clung to the heat of the day, thick with dust, smoke, and the scent of overripe fruit and horse sweat.

Galdon stepped out into the waning light like a man emerging from the grave. He stretched his arms wide, face tilted upward, and groaned as the warmth kissed the chill from his damp bones.

"By stone and forge, that feels good."

The wizard paused beside him, squinting against the sun as if it offended him.

"I thought dwarves preferred the dark. Subterranean creatures and all." The words dripped with disdain.

Galdon snorted and rolled his shoulders.

"Bah! That?" He jerked a thumb toward the dungeon entrance behind them. "That's not underground. That's a rot pit with a roof. A proper dwarven hall is dry, carved with care, heated by the fires of the forge, and lit with gemstone lanterns. Not slime and mildew."

The wizard arched one brow in visible surprise — whether at being corrected or at the unexpected poetry of the dwarf's words was unclear. But the moment passed quickly, and his face hardened again.

"Come," he said curtly. And so they walked.

They descended through the city's layers like water trickling into a deep well—each street a little rougher, each turn a little darker. The higher districts glittered in the fading light, their market stalls folding like golden flowers at dusk, merchants counting coins and chattering about profits. Children ran home with bread tucked under arms and mischief under their fingernails.

But that was above.

They were going down.

Soon, the cobbled stones beneath their boots gave way to rougher paths—cracked bricks, then dry-packed earth. The lanterns grew fewer and farther between. What light there was flickered, more ash than flame, casting long shadows from figures who didn't care to be seen.

By the time they reached the city's lowest quarter, night had fully claimed the streets. The only people around were those who lived by it. Eyes watched from alleyways, some curious, some hungry. Laughter echoed faintly from windows left open to let in air, sharp, hollow laughter with no warmth in it. Galdon kept one hand near the dagger tucked beneath his tattered vest, though he doubted it would do much. And beside him, the wizard walked as though nothing in this place could touch him. He may have been right. Then they saw it.

The Watering Hole.

Its sign dangled from one hinge, swinging with a rusty creak in the warm breeze. The letters were faded and nearly illegible, though the painted mug below had been updated with fresh vomit at some point in recent history.

Laughter roared from within, thick and slurred. The kind of place where knives were more common than napkins, and the drinks tasted like regret and fungal root.

Galdon stopped in his tracks. There hung a sign, "The Grimy Mug."

"Oh no," he groaned. "Not here. This place has a smell. I performed here once, and the barmaid offered to pay me not to come back."

The wizard's mouth twisted.

"Yes. Here. The people I need you to see will be here. And you will receive your final instructions."

He said it like the final instructions might come with an undertaker. Galdon stared at the crooked doorway, the burst of noise and sour air wafting out with every swing of the door.

"This is how it starts, then?" he muttered.

The wizard turned toward him.

"Yes. With dirt, sweat, and beer that doubles as cleaning fluid. Now," he gestured with a mocking flourish. "Shall we?"

And Galdon, knowing deep down that it would only get worse from here, squared his shoulders and stepped through the door of the Watering Hole.

He was right.

Chapter Eight: The Mission and the Minotaur

The wizard paused at the tavern entrance and gave Galdon a polite nod that somehow still dripped with superiority.

"After you."

Galdon didn't argue. Not because he wanted to, but because the smell of the place was already starting to burn the inside of his nose, and hesitating meant breathing more of it.

He ducked his head as low as dignity allowed, doing his best not to be noticed. Being the dwarf dragged out by city guards the night before wasn't exactly the kind of fame that earned you applause in places like The Grimy Mug, more commonly referred to by locals as simply "the Grime," which, Galdon noted bitterly as they stepped inside, was entirely appropriate.

The place was loud. And rank. And full of people who seemed to have just lost something: their last coin, their patience, or their grip on consciousness. Some of them had clearly lost all three.

He made for the farthest table from the bar—half in shadow, half sticky—and slouched into the seat with the air of a man trying to disappear into a wall.

The wizard followed without comment, taking the opposite chair and flagging down a server with one raised brow. Moments later, two mugs of what passed for beer were thudded onto the table. The liquid inside sloshed like it resented being disturbed.

The wizard lifted his mug with casual disdain and took a sip. Galdon did the same. And nearly choked.

"Sweet stone, what is this?" he sputtered.

"Authentic," the wizard replied dryly.

Galdon grumbled and wiped his mouth. Then he froze. The man across from him… was not the same. At least, not in appearance.

The once-imposing wizard, the sharp-jawed shadow who had descended into the dungeon with fire in his eyes, now looked like a perfectly forgettable commoner—slightly hunched, slightly greasy, slightly unremarkable in every possible way. Even his hair was different. Grayer. Thinner. The transformation was uncanny.

Galdon stared.

"How… when did you—?"

The wizard chuckled. Low and cold.

"You don't look like you either, dwarf. You're welcome."

Galdon's hand shot up to his beard. He hadn't noticed the minor alterations—less braid, less bush, more street-level "don't-look-at-me" flavor.

"I'm a grandmaster of my craft," the wizard said, savoring the words like a good insult. "Your astonishment is mildly insulting."

He set his mug down and leaned in, eyes sharp.

"Now. To business."

Galdon rolled his eyes.

"This should be good."

"You see that table? Over there. Left of the hearth. Look carefully."

Galdon followed his gaze.

There they sat:

- A Minotaur slumped in his chair, and a mug balanced precariously on his gut, his armor dented in more places than Galdon could count.

- A young man—likely human—gesturing wildly with his hands, a faint spark flickering from his fingertips every few seconds like a firefly with indigestion.

- And a gnome, who appeared to be having an intense argument with a bowl of peanuts.

Galdon blinked.

"Sounds like the start of a bad joke," he muttered. "A minotaur, a gnome, and a mage walk into a bar…"

The wizard didn't smile.

"Pay attention, dwarf. I don't enjoy repeating myself."

Galdon gave him a look. The wizard gave it right back.

"Those three," he said, gesturing subtly, "are your traveling companions. You are to infiltrate their group, earn their trust, and retrieve two things: a trinket—Minotaur-shaped, carved with arcane symbols—and a map. Those two items are the key to your task."

Galdon raised an eyebrow.

"You want me to steal from them?"

"Befriend them," the wizard corrected, though the curl in his lip said he didn't care how it was done. "I suspect they'll be more useful than you believe. And they already have the items you need."

Galdon snorted.

"Useful? That Minotaur can barely sit upright. He looks like he arm-wrestled a donkey and lost. The human mage's spellwork last night

nearly caught the table on fire while ordering soup. And the gnome…
what good is a gnome? Especially one who's losing an argument to
salted legumes?"

The wizard leaned back, folding his hands.

"Nevertheless. This is your task."

Galdon rubbed his forehead and groaned.

"Why is it always me?"

The wizard raised his mug in mock cheer.

"Because you're expendable."

The wizard reached into the folds of his cloak—no longer a regal
garment of mystic prestige, but now a patchy, soot-gray robe that
smelled faintly of burnt parsley—and retrieved a small pouch. It jingled
with promise as he set it gently on the table between them.

Galdon's eyes flicked to it, then back to the wizard's face,
suspicious.

"You'll need supplies," the wizard said quietly, the firelight
flickering in his eyes, "use these coins wisely. There won't be more."

Galdon raised a brow. "No advance pay, no hazard bonus, and now
you're putting me on a budget?"

The wizard didn't laugh.

He simply leaned closer.

"Find me in the Master's Tower upon your return. Ask for
Grandmaster Landro. Do not fail me."

It wasn't a request. It wasn't even a threat. It was a sentence,
delivered like stone, falling into water—calm, inevitable, and bound to
cause ripples.

Then, without another word, Landro stood. He adjusted his worn traveler's cloak with an absent flick of the wrist, gave Galdon one last lingering look, a look filled with warning, certainty, and the kind of pressure that made lesser men fold—and walked out of the Watering Hole.

No one stopped him. No one even looked twice. The tavern swallowed him whole. Galdon sat back in his chair, eyes on the swinging tavern door, the pouch of coins suddenly heavier than it had any right to be. From the alley outside, the night seemed to pause. And somewhere, far above the dingy streets, Grandmaster Landro allowed himself a smirk. Not the smug grin of a man who had outwitted a thief. But the smile of someone who had just lit a slow-burning fuse and was already walking away.

"Failure," he murmured to himself, as the city lights shimmered below, "would not be advisable."

Chapter Nine: Staff, Sparks, and the Frog Incident

Micah Metcalf skipped merrily along the dusty path, his robes flapping around his ankles like they were trying to flee his fashion sense. His staff, a crooked length of ash wood that had once belonged to a wizard of moderate repute and inferior balance, tapped in rhythm with his steps.

Tap. Tap. Tappa-tap.

Each bounce of the staff sent up a small puff of dirt, and Micah grinned at the sun as if it had personally invited him out for the day.

This was it—his first real adventure.

No teachers.

No detentions.

No mop duty for accidentally reanimating the library's dust collection. Just him, his spells (most of which probably worked), and the open road. He gave a little hop and spun once, arms wide.

"Take that, Master Goldwyn!" he declared to the empty sky.

The sky, for its part, remained silent. Possibly terrified. He chuckled at the memory of that morning's catastrophe—the final straw, so to speak. It had started with an "innocent" alchemy experiment in Master Goldwyn's classroom. Micah had been trying to transmute powdered iron into floating lanterns. What he got instead was a rapid ignition reaction, three airborne cauldrons, and a string of flaming scrolls that spiraled across the ceiling like very determined fireworks.

He could still see the expression on Master Goldwyn's face, once the smoke had cleared and his eyebrows had stopped smoldering. It had been a mixture of awe and horror. Mostly horror.

"It was only a small fire," Micah muttered to himself. "And the floor was barely scorched. Mostly."

He shrugged and kept walking.

"Besides, they weren't teaching me anything useful anyway. Always the same spells, the same books, the same crusty toads droning on about restraint and structure."

He shuddered at the memory of Professor Thumble's lecture on "magical etiquette in royal court environments." It had lasted four hours and included a detailed demonstration of napkin folding. And then there was the Great Frog Shower. Now that had been a highlight.

The morning sky had opened up without warning, and down came frogs. Hundreds of them. Plop. Splash. Splop. Students had screamed, sprinted, slipped, and swore. The courtyard turned into a slippery, croaking chaos. Micah had watched it all from behind a pillar, trying very hard not to laugh. He succeeded for about twelve seconds.

That afternoon, the academy buzzed with wild rumors.

"It was a curse!"

"A prank from the illusionists!"

"It's a prophecy!"

"I think the frogs were trying to tell us something."

Micah, of course, said nothing.

But the smile tugging at his lips betrayed him—a grin equal parts mischievous and proud. He might have tested a weather alteration spell in the early hours. And he might have accidentally swapped "mist" for "amphibious precipitation." And he definitely hadn't told anyone. But no one got hurt. And it was spectacular.

Now here he was, wand in his pocket, staff in hand, eyes on the horizon, and not a single adult in sight to stop him. Adventure had officially begun. And somewhere, far behind him, the academy's charred roof tiles still bore faint scorch marks in the shape of his initials.

Later that same fateful day, as if the frog storm hadn't cemented his legacy well enough, another incident rippled through the academy halls. This one was slimier.

The Headmaster's voice—usually measured and grave like the toll of an ancient bell—had risen to a dramatic, almost squealing register as he bellowed across the polished stone corridors.

"WHO PUT SLUGS IN MY BED?!?!"

The question echoed from floor to vaulted floor, chasing students into classrooms and hiding spots alike. Micah, tucked comfortably in the shadow of a seldom-used alcove behind a tapestry of the First Elven Accord (featuring unusually judgmental-looking unicorns), grinned with silent satisfaction.

He didn't confirm he was responsible. He didn't deny it either. Besides, it had been a very dull morning, and the slugs had already been enchanted to sing in harmony when touched. A gift, really.

He waited until the sound of frantic cleaning staff and the headmaster's sputtering indignation faded, then slipped out with the stealth of a very smug alley cat.

"I did manage to get a cool map before I left, though," Micah mused aloud, patting the pocket of his satchel. "Not that I need it. I'm already a natural adventurer. But maybe I'll trade it for something useful… like a pie. Or pants with fewer burn holes."

He whistled as he walked, the breeze ruffling his hair and the trees whispering secrets he couldn't quite understand. The open road greeted him with birdsong, the scent of blooming thyme, and a distinct lack of authority figures.

Life was good.

Until it wasn't.

Up ahead, the cheerful sounds of the forest were marred by sharp laughter and the unmistakable whimper of something small in distress.

Micah's steps quickened.

In a clearing just off the path, he spotted them: three scrappy children, none older than ten, circling a trembling little rabbit. The creature's fur was muddy, its ears back, its eyes wide.

Micah frowned.

"Oi!" he called out, marching toward them.

The children startled—two stepped back, defensive. The third crossed his arms, as if daring this strange young man with wild hair and a crooked staff to say something unwise.

Micah reached into his pouch.

His fingers brushed across a blue feather—long and shimmering, with veins of iridescent silver that caught the sun like spun sapphire. A relic from a failed (but fabulous) summoning lesson. He hadn't meant to pull a griffon's grooming feather, but here they were.

He pulled it out with a flourish, letting the sunlight catch its gleam.

The children froze.

The most petite boy stepped forward, his earlier bravado gone, replaced by wide-eyed wonder.

"Is that… a griffon feather?" he whispered.

Micah knelt, lowering the feather like a royal scepter.

"The very same," he said solemnly. "Plucked from the underwing of the Azure Roamer himself during a mid-air duel above Mount Wyrmfang."

The children gasped. Even the muddy one with the snarl melted a little.

"You fought a griffon?"

Micah smiled.

"We… disagreed over a seating arrangement—long story. But—" he held the feather just out of reach, "I'm willing to trade. One genuine, enchanted griffon feather... in exchange for leaving that rabbit alone and maybe helping him find a snack instead of scaring the ears off him."

The children huddled.

After a moment, the self-appointed leader turned back, nodded, and held out his hand.

"Deal."

Micah handed over the feather with a grin. The rabbit blinked up at him as if unsure whether to run or nominate him for sainthood.

"Run along, little buddy," Micah whispered.

The rabbit bolted.

The children, now crowded around their prize, whispered with reverence.

As Micah turned back to the road, he couldn't help but glance down at his staff, then at the clouds overhead.

"See? Responsible adventuring. I can totally do this."

He'd nearly forgotten the map again. But it was still tucked safely in his bag.

The rabbit stopped and hid to watch what was happening.

But indeed," Micah nodded, slipping into the smooth, theatrical voice he'd been practicing in front of the mirror since he was eight. He let a shadow of mystery creep into his tone, adding just the right touch of wizardly gravitas. "It's said to bring good luck to those who treat creatures with kindness."

The children stood frozen for a moment, feather clutched in awe, as if expecting the skies to split or a unicorn to descend. Instead, there was only a beat of silence, broken by the rustle of dry grass and the sound of one of them slowly exhaling.

Then, after a whispered huddle, the children nodded and stepped back. The rabbit blinked, nose twitching, before disappearing into the forest like a whisper of wind through leaves.

Micah watched it go with satisfaction.

One small victory.

He turned back to the children and tucked his staff under his arm.

"Tell me, brave adventurers," he said, brushing dirt from his robes with a flourish, "what village lies ahead on this noble road? For I am parched, and the hour grows desperate. I require… ale."

One of the children, a gangly boy with freckles and a perpetual squint, stepped forward.

"Swine View," he said. "That's the next village. Just over the hill."

Micah blinked.

"Swine View?"

He mouthed the name silently, eyebrows rising.

What a peculiar name.

Probably full of pigs. Or people who snort when they laugh.

"Excellent," he declared, though his voice held a tiny crack of doubt.

"I shall refresh myself in this fine establishment. Hopefully not with swine."

But then a sudden and troubling realization struck him.

He checked his satchel.

No coin.

Not a single shimmering shard of silver or copper.

Just a few suspiciously sticky pieces of toffee and a crushed acorn from a squirrel he'd tried to befriend last week.

His eyes brightened.

"Say… would you like to see some magic?"

The children perked up, immediately suspicious.

"Real magic?" the smallest asked, eyes narrowing.

Micah puffed his chest and placed a hand over his heart.

"Real magic. For a small price, I will dazzle you with a performance so magnificent it may cause temporary blindness due to sheer amazement."

The children huddled again.

More whispering. More sideways glances.

Finally, the oldest—the appointed negotiator—stepped forward and fished a single coin from his pocket.

"Okay. One coin. Dazzle us."

Micah accepted it with the gravity of a king receiving tribute.

"Prepare yourselves," he said, and stepped back with a flourish.

He cracked his knuckles, adjusted his sleeves, and twirled his staff overhead.

This was it.

The trick he'd been working on for months. The one he hadn't dared try during classes after the incident with the floating latrines—a controlled illusion spell—simple in theory, elegant in execution.

He inhaled deeply.

"Smoke of stars, light of night, gather round and grant them fright!"

He clapped his hands, pointed his staff to the sky…

And produced a mild puff.

Not a grand illusion. Not a spiral of color or the shimmering silhouette of a phoenix.

Just… a tiny, confused wisp of mist, the sort of thing a sleepy teapot might cough up on a lazy Sunday.

The mist hovered.

Wobbled.

And drifted directly into one of the children's faces, who coughed politely.

A long silence followed.

Micah's eyes widened in horror.

He forced a grin. "Ah-ha! The subtlety of the spell! It is… nuanced!"

Another awkward pause.

Then one of the boys leaned over to the others and whispered:

"Did he just summon fog?"

"It smelled like socks," another replied.

Micah cleared his throat and did a dramatic bow anyway.

"Thank you, noble patrons. You've been a magnificent audience."

The children exchanged glances, then shrugged.

"Got anything else?" the smallest one asked.

Micah blinked.

Then smiled sheepishly.

"Only… interpretive dance."

"Ew."

Undeterred by the cough-inducing wisp of magical fog that had floated directly into a child's face, Micah brushed off his robes, lifted his chin, and said with renewed vigor:

"Now, for my next trick!"

He rummaged through his satchel and pulled out a wooden spoon—worn, slightly singed at the edges, and absolutely enchanted. Probably. Maybe. Hopefully.

He held it up like a relic from a long-lost culinary order.

"Behold! The Levitating Spoon of Eldemire the Whisker!" he declared.

The children—still skeptical but now morbidly curious—crossed their arms.

Micah narrowed his eyes, whispered an incantation under his breath, and made a series of dramatic gestures that could have been spellwork or extremely expressive swatting.

The spoon wobbled.

It twitched.

It rose.

A full inch.

"Yes!" Micah cried.

And then it fell.

Clatter.

"Ah," he said, smiling through the pain. "That… was part of it. The dramatic fall! Very symbolic."

The children were not impressed.

One of them began to shake his head. Another mimed falling asleep on the grass.

Micah wiped a bead of sweat from his brow and held up a single, shining coin—the one the children had given him.

"But now," he said with a theatrical whisper, "for my grand finale. The transformation of a coin into a dove. Witness the miraculous metamorphosis from wealth to wonder!"

He took a deep breath. Closed his eyes. Gathered all the arcane knowledge rattling around in his skull, the kind that had once summoned both soap bubbles and bats.

He whispered, chanted, flicked his fingers, and dropped the coin dramatically into his palm.

The children leaned in.

The coin shivered.

It trembled.

And then—

Plop.

It fell to the grass.

Still a coin.

Not even a feathery coin.

Micah stared at it.

The silence was louder than any gasp could've been.

The kids' faces changed from amusement to suspicion. Suspicion to irritation.

And then—to Micah's slowly dawning horror—to unified purpose.

"Get him."

The words were spoken with the precise, cold resolve of small warriors wronged.

"Wait! Wait, wait, wait!" Micah cried, taking one cautious step back.

But it was too late.

The horde descended.

With all the speed and chaotic energy of a pack of sugar-fueled puppies, the children tackled him to the ground.

Micah yelped as grubby hands fumbled through his satchel, pockets, and sleeves with professional pickpocket enthusiasm.

"Hey! Not the robe—this was school-issued!"

"That's my toffee!"

"Don't pull that—OH, that's attached!"

He flailed, wriggled, and squealed, but the little marauders were relentless.

Despite Micah's increasingly theatrical protests—complete with exaggerated yelps, flailing arms, and shrill cries of "Mercy! I am but a humble wizard!"—he was quickly and thoroughly overwhelmed.

The children, emboldened by shared grievance and the scent of victory, swarmed him with the practiced efficiency of seasoned pickpockets.

Micah, who wasn't exactly towering over anyone to begin with, found himself flattened, flustered, and flung to the mercy of a tiny tribunal armed with sticky fingers and a unified mission: retrieve the coin.

They dove into his cloak, rummaged through his pockets, and examined every suspicious-looking pouch, pulling out everything from lint and beetle shells to a crumpled spell of mild headache relief.

"That's not a map—it's a menu!"

"This toffee's got lint on it!"

"Is this a feather or part of a mop?"

Micah squealed with exaggerated desperation.

"Help! HELP! I'm under siege by a battalion of sugar-fueled barbarians!"

"Whoa, whoa, whoa, what's going on here?"

A firm but friendly voice cut through the chaos.

One by one, the children were disentangled, gently dusted off, and set upright.

The speaker stood above Micah now, arms crossed, one eyebrow raised. Sunlight glinted off the metal bracers on his arms, and his broad frame suggested someone who'd lifted more than a few barrels in his day.

Micah blinked up at him from the grass.

The stranger chuckled warmly and extended a firm but unthreatening hand.

"Up you get, would-be wizard. Maybe work on your magic—or your negotiation skills—next time."

Micah took the offered hand, letting himself be hoisted upright with all the dramatic flair of a man rising from the ashes. Grass clung to his robes. A twig poked out of his hair at a comically heroic angle.

The children, now victorious and coin-in-hand, scampered off into the distance, no doubt already planning their next coup against a lemonade vendor or stray chicken.

The stranger brushed a bit of dirt from Micah's shoulder with a surprisingly gentle hand, and that's when Micah finally got a proper look at him.

And the first thing he noticed was the nose.

It was… magnificent. Vast. Majestic. Like a topographical landmark, one might spot it on a cartographer's map.

"Wow," Micah blurted, eyes wide. "That's sure big. Does it weigh your head down?"

A beat of silence followed.

Micah blinked, realized what he'd said, and quickly added:

"Pardon me, thank you for saving me. I'm Micah! A most extraordinary wizard." He bowed slightly, almost tripping over his staff.

The stranger—whose expression had turned very still—grasped his hand with a single firm pump.

"Sniffles," he said evenly. "And no, it does not weigh my head down." His eyes narrowed just enough to suggest that perhaps Micah's head ought to weigh a little more.

Micah, sensing the possibility of having immediately offended his savior, scrambled for a distraction.

"You're a gnome! I've never met one in person before. How incredible!"

Sniffles raised an eyebrow.

"Really? Have you been hiding under a rock?"

Micah gasped. "Good heavens, no! Why would I do that? Rocks are cold. And hard. And heavy! I imagine it would flatten me like a pancake. Honestly, it seems like a poor choice for a hideout."

Sniffles stared at him.

Long and hard.

This one was definitely dropped as a baby. Maybe twice.

He sighed. "Right. Okay then."

Before further gaffes could tumble from Micah's lips, the young wizard looped an arm through Sniffles' and began steering him toward the town gates with enthusiastic energy and zero spatial awareness.

"Come! You saved me from the clutching claws of chaos. I owe you ale, or at least something fizzy."

Sniffles, bewildered but not unamused, allowed himself to be guided.

The Muddy Puddle (of questionable origin)

The tavern in Swine View was a delightful mess—a maelstrom of laughter, clinking tankards, the sizzle of grease, and the unmistakable scent of stewed onions and well-worn boots.

They found a cozy corner table under a crooked beam and settled in.

Micah gestured wildly as he regaled Sniffles with tales of magical mayhem, casting invisible spells that occasionally startled waitstaff and once lit a candle three tables away. Sniffles, in turn, shared travel stories with the dry wit of someone who'd seen far too much and lived to roll his eyes about it.

The pair laughed, argued about the philosophical implications of enchanted biscuits, and debated whether dragons could be ticklish.

The longer the evening stretched, the more their rhythm synced.

Micah's chaos.

Sniffles' sarcasm.

Together, it worked.

And from that moment on, they were inseparable.

An unlikely duo:

Sniffles, the long-nosed gnome with clever hands and quiet wisdom.

Micah, the bubbling cauldron of wonder and accidental combustion.

Rarely was one seen without the other.

And in the years to come, their friendship would become legendary.

If not for their heroism…

In the years to come, for the trail of bewildered bartenders, exploded soup bowls, and unexplained poultry incidents left in their wake, their names would be whispered with reverence, or at least laughter, in taverns across the realm.

Micah and Sniffles.

The wizard who couldn't quite cast, and the gnome whose nose could sniff out both trouble and strong drink from half a league away.

Their favorite haunt became The Watering Hole, of course. They had options—places with flashier drinks and louder tunes—but familiarity always pulled them back. The Watering Hole wasn't just a bar; it was their haven, a place steeped in shared memories, where their laughter lingered in the air and the walls had long become keepers of their stories.

And that is where they headed next.

There, surrounded by splintered tables, greasy platters, and enough spilled ale to flood a cellar, they felt most at home. Night after night, the two could be found in their favorite booth—half-listening to local gossip while Micah occasionally tried to set it to music (badly) and Sniffles tried not to fall asleep mid-complaint.

It was during one of these particularly frothy evenings—when their mugs had been topped off more times than either could count—that they overheard a grizzled traveler whispering to another patron.

"Burnin' the trees, I tell you. Nymphs are beside themselves. Some gang's been slicing off limbs, scorchin' bark, laughin' while doin' it. Offered a reward, they did. Anyone who helps the forest folk."

The man's companion scoffed.

"Who's fool enough to get involved with tree nymph politics?"

Micah stood up. Dramatically.

"We are."

He swayed only a little.

Sniffles blinked up at him, bleary-eyed.

"We are?"

"We are," Micah nodded solemnly. "For coin. And justice. And maybe snacks."

The traveler squinted.

"You serious?"

"Deadly," Micah said, nearly falling into the soup.

They never made it far.

They made it precisely to the stables, where they collapsed into a mound of straw and horse dung, fully dressed for glory.

The last thing Micah remembered was Sniffles humming something tuneless about "defending bark with bravery" and trying to toast to a horse.

The morning after

Micah groaned awake with the grace of a collapsing shelf. His head throbbed like a drum solo gone wrong. Blinking through crusted eyes, he realized—with a mix of confusion and revulsion—that his nose was pressed firmly against a sock.

A sock.

Attached to Sniffles.

Sniffles' feet had served as Micah's makeshift pillow during the night's descent into chaos. And not just any part—the toes.

He raised his head slowly, trying not to disturb the creature attached to said sock.

Sniffles was snoring.

Loudly.

Each inhale drew in a panicked fly, which whirled in circles before being blown back out on the exhale, its wings ruffled, its dignity shredded.

Micah blinked. The fly blinked (probably). Then it zipped off into the rising sun as if it had seen things no fly should see.

Gingerly, Micah stood.

Sniffles groaned and sat up, a blob of straw and something unspeakable clinging to his cheek. He peeled it off without looking and muttered darkly.

"I am never drinking dwarf spirits again."

Micah rolled his eyes.

"You say that every time."

Sniffles scratched his chin.

"Well, maybe this time I mean it."

Micah turned and spotted a crumpled piece of parchment half-buried in the straw pile. He picked it up, shook it out, and then shook it again—this time for dung.

He squinted.

"Looks like… directions?"

Sniffles leaned over.

"Oh no."

"Oh yes?"

Sniffles rubbed his temple.

"I remember now. The tree nymphs. We promised to help save their forest from a band of tree-burning hooligans."

Micah whimpered.

"Why would we do that?"

"We had bellies full of liquid courage," Sniffles muttered, eyes distant with the horror of remembered bravado.

"So we gave our word?"

Sniffles nodded solemnly.

"And you threw in a lifetime supply of hugs if they carved your name in a tree."

Micah slapped a hand to his face.

"Well, then. We're doomed. Might as well be noble about it."

After a quick rinse and a lot of gagging, the pair returned to the tavern long enough to stock up on travel supplies—purchased with the last of Sniffles' remaining coinage and Micah's relentless charm (read: awkward haggling and mild begging).

The path wound through the landscape like a serpentine riddle, twisting between overgrown hedges, dipping under low-hanging branches, and occasionally disappearing entirely beneath creeping moss. It was narrow, uneven, and far too enthusiastic about turning ankles.

Micah, of course, was delighted.

He was far more focused on the vibrant flora brushing at the edges of the trail than the treacherous ground beneath his boots. Every few paces, he gasped and pointed excitedly at something utterly ordinary—a crooked mushroom, a fluttering leaf, a suspiciously shaped rock he was sure was enchanted.

"Look at that vine! I think it blinked!"

"That's poison ivy, Micah," Sniffles grunted without looking.

Micah immediately yanked his hand back and wiped it frantically on his robe.

Lost in wide-eyed wonder, the young wizard tripped over a half-buried root for what must have been the tenth time. He pinwheeled forward—

—And once again, Sniffles caught him.

"Watch out!" the gnome barked, steadying him by the belt.

He chuckled as he let go. "The forest tests your mettle before you even meet the nymphs. At this rate, you'll faceplant into diplomacy."

"I'm adding 'forest root' to my list of natural enemies," Micah muttered, rubbing his shin. "Just below flying soup bowls."

The sun, meanwhile, had become their least favorite travel companion.

It beat down relentlessly, turning the air into a shimmering curtain of heat that clung to their skin like a damp, judgmental spell. Dust rose with every step, sticking to their clothes, their faces, their teeth. It swirled around their heads and attacked their eyes with gleeful precision, making each blink feel like a gritty gamble.

Sniffles walked with his hat pulled low, sweat clinging to his brow and nose like condensation on a teapot. His mood was slowly deteriorating to match the trail—thorny, sharp, and full of hidden frustrations.

The pebbles underfoot weren't so much a surface as a personal vendetta.

"Remind me again," Sniffles growled, "why we're marching into a forest known for its allure, not its footpaths?"

Micah, still peering at a glittering beetle with absolute wonder, replied absent-mindedly:

"Because justice never takes the paved road."

Sniffles made a sound somewhere between a grunt and a groan.

"No, but apparently justice is ankle-deep in tiny rocks and smells faintly of horse dung and bad ideas."

As they rounded a bend, the undergrowth grew thicker, the light filtered through in dappled patterns, and the sounds of the forest shifted—birdsong dimming, wind rustling quieter, like the woods were holding their breath.

Micah stopped, lifting a hand.

Sniffles blinked.

"What?"

"I think… we're getting close."

Sniffles adjusted his pack, muttering something about tree-huggers and misplaced optimism, but even he couldn't shake the feeling that the air itself was changing.

The magic was getting stronger.

The forest deepened.

The sunlight now filtered in like whispered secrets—muted gold slicing through a canopy of emerald. The air had shifted from sweltering to strange, laced with the scent of jasmine and wet bark. The dust had mercifully vanished, replaced by loamy moss that muffled their footsteps with suspicious hospitality.

Micah walked slower now, eyes wide with wonder. He turned slowly in a circle, letting his fingers brush low-hanging vines.

"It's enchanted," he whispered, awestruck. "You can feel it. The trees are alive with it."

Sniffles glanced up at the nearest trunk.

"They're trees, Micah. Of course they're alive."

"No, no," Micah said, pausing to press his ear to the bark of a particularly gnarled oak. "Alive-alive. Like… sentient. Probably fluent in Forest Tongue."

Sniffles stopped walking.

"Forest. Tongue."

Micah nodded solemnly.

"I studied a bit. Just in case. I'm going to try to communicate."

"Oh no."

Before Sniffles could intervene, Micah stepped up to the tree, raised his staff dramatically, cleared his throat, and proclaimed:

"O leafy one! Gnarled sovereign of the barked realm! Speak to me, your wand-wielding son of the wind!"

He then made a series of guttural clicks and whooshing noises.

Sniffles stared.

The forest was silent. So very silent.

Then—SNAP.

A vine whipped up from the ground, caught Micah by the ankle, and yanked him off his feet with comedic enthusiasm. His hat spun in the air like a startled bird.

"AUGH! I HAVE ANGERED THE TREE GODS!"

Sniffles did not move. He folded his arms and sighed.

"Micah, you said it had 'the odor of wet cheese' and then insulted its bark pigmentation."

Micah dangled upside down from the tree, spinning slowly like a confused piñata.

"It's not my fault! Forest Tongue is a tonal language!"

Sniffles walked over and yanked out his dagger. With a few careful slices, the vine gave a dramatic shudder and released Micah, who landed in a soft puff of moss—and a not-so-soft thunk of pride.

He sat up, hair full of leaves, eyes wide.

"I think… that was a test."

"No, Micah," Sniffles said, sheathing his dagger. "That was you declaring war on foliage."

A rustle echoed overhead, and something giggled.

Soft, musical, and far too mischievous to be wind.

Micah and Sniffles froze.

"Did you hear that?"

"Yes," Sniffles said, eyes scanning the trees. "And I have a bad feeling our audience just got a lot more… thug shaped."

"Okay!" Micah said in his bravest, not-at-all-squeaky voice, puffing out his chest as he gripped his staff. "Let's find these bullies and get done with them, shall we?"

Inside, of course, he was trembling like a startled jellyfish.

Sniffles, ever the realist, sighed through his nose—which, to be fair, was a lot of sighs—and trudged after his friend deeper into the forest.

They didn't get far.

Just as the trees began to arch overhead into an emerald cathedral, the sounds of voices filtered through the leaves—sharp, muffled, and not speaking in friendly tones.

Sniffles stopped cold.

Micah, entirely preoccupied with following an exquisite butterfly that dared to sparkle mid-air, didn't notice—and crashed directly into Sniffles' back, knocking the poor gnome face-first into the moss.

"Oops! Sorry, Sniffles," Micah whispered, kneeling beside him. "I was otherwise engaged with, erm, aerial entomology."

Sniffles hissed and waved for him to get down.

"Shush! I hear voices," he whispered, tapping his ear.

Micah blinked and scooted back.

"I'm sure we can find a healer for you," he said sincerely, eyes darting left and right. "Maybe there's a druid clinic around—"

"Not in my head, you dolt!" Sniffles snapped. "Over there!" He pointed sharply to the left.

Micah relaxed, wiping a dramatic bead of sweat from his brow.

"Whew. You had me worried for a moment. Thought you were going full bard on me."

A twig snapped behind them.

Both froze.

Then—WHUMP.

Two burlap bags were flung down over their heads.

"HEY—WHAT—WHO—MMPH!"

Before they could so much as squawk a protest, both were hoisted like sacks of flour and thrown overboard, not-at-all-friendly shoulders.

"Oomph!" they grunted in unison as their respective captors jostled down a narrow path.

When they were unceremoniously dumped on the forest floor, the air was knocked from their lungs, and their dignity flew somewhere into the canopy.

Within moments, they were tied back to back, arms pinned behind them, and their head sacks yanked off with dramatic flair.

Both gasped.

"My goodness," Micah wheezed. "That was stuffy in there, wasn't it, Sniffles? Felt like breathing through a badger's sock."

Sniffles ignored him and wiggled furiously.

"Oh, hello there!" Micah said with a nervous smile, his voice shooting up an octave. "If you would be so kind as to untie us, we'd be right on our way. You see, we've been charged—very official and everything—with the disposal of some mean thugs bothering the local tree nymphs, and we're running… ever so slightly late."

Sniffles, tied back-to-back with him, let out a frantic grunt and began jerking his shoulder against Micah's—desperate Morse code.

Micah turned his head.

"What is it? Do you have an itch?"

Another shoulder thump. More frantic.

Micah's brow furrowed. Then, slowly, realization dawned across his face like a doomed sunrise.

His expression crumpled.

"Oh."

He turned back to the towering brute looming over them.

"Well, umm…" he stammered, color draining from his cheeks, "I'm sure they're very nice thugs. Very misunderstood. Probably victims of social bias. We've decided to—erm—not pursue them. We were just discussing a full retreat when you so thoughtfully threw those absolutely revolting bags over our heads."

The large human standing before them—broad-shouldered, grease-smudged, and wearing armor that looked like it had been stolen from a scarecrow—stared at Micah with mild disbelief.

Then he grinned.

An evil, toothy, definitely-hasn't-seen-a-dentist grin.

"Well, well," he drawled, stepping closer, his boots crunching over dry leaves. "A pair of would-be heroes. I'm afraid, little maggots, that we are not nice thugs. Nor are we particularly understanding. We burn understanding. And pee on nice."

Micah winced. "That's a very confusing metaphor."

"Shut up."

The brute reached down, pulled a rag from his belt—one that had seen far too many meals and no soap—and shoved it squarely into Micah's mouth.

"MMPH!"

Sniffles didn't fare any better. He got what might have been someone's old sock.

Gagged and glaring, the two were left squirming while the thugs returned to their fire, snickering.

The lead thug threw more wood on the flames and warmed his hands.

"We'll decide the most painful way to eliminate them after supper," he said casually. "Maybe something with ants."

Micah and Sniffles exchanged wide-eyed glances.

Sniffles was wriggling furiously, trying to work at the knots. Nothing gave. His face was turning red—not with fear, but with sheer gnomish indignation.

Micah slumped. A muffled whimper escaped through his gag.

And then… a whisper on the wind.

Soft. Melodic. Laced with magic.

A breeze passed through the clearing, unnatural and cool.

The thugs froze.

Something shimmered behind the firelight.

A set of glowing eyes blinked from the treetops.

Then—giggles.

The forest began to hum.

And something else was watching now.

Micah sat slumped, awkwardly gagged, bound, and faced with the growing realization that he and Sniffles were most likely going to end their adventuring careers as roach bait. He sighed through his nose. Loudly. Twice.

Across the fire, the thugs laughed boisterously, utterly unaware of the growing tension in the woods around them.

Micah glanced around in defeat, his gaze sweeping across the forest's edge, and stopped.

His eyes widened.

There, nestled in the underbrush, was a small, familiar figure. Fluffy, wide-eyed, and nibbling on a leaf like it hadn't a care in the world.

The rabbit.

The very same one Micah had rescued from the child mob back in Swine View.

But it wasn't alone.

Behind it, wings shimmered.

Dozens—no, hundreds—of tiny, iridescent wings.

Fairies.

They flickered into view like living stars, swirling in the firelight like glitter caught in a whirlwind. Their laughter was like wind chimes, full of mischief. Their eyes sparkled with a delight that meant someone was about to regret their life choices.

The rabbit, ever the unsung hero, hopped right up to Micah and began chewing at the ropes binding his wrists. Sniffles wriggled beside him, gagged, but trying to shout something that sounded suspiciously like, "IS THAT THE RABBIT YOU TOLD ME ABOUT?"

Micah could only blink in grateful awe as the ropes began to loosen.

Meanwhile, the thugs—brutal, grimy, and proud members of the "We Only Believe in Hitting Things" Union—froze mid-laugh.

One by one, they turned to see a cloud of glowing, winged figures spiraling toward them.

Delicate.

Dazzling.

Deadly adorable.

"Wh-what the—" one stammered, taking a step back.

Another gasped, hand clutching his axe like a child gripping a teddy bear in a thunderstorm.

"F-Fairies?" someone whispered.

"Those aren't real!"

"They're in my hair!!"

The fairies swirled closer, their tiny hands tugging on ears, untying belts, and tickling under armpits with the merciless joy of magical pranksters.

The bravado of hardened thuggery crumpled like a wet scroll.

"RUN!" one shrieked, his voice cracking into soprano.

And just like that, they scattered—a chaotic whirlwind of terror and dropped weapons, fleeing into the undergrowth like toddlers running from bath time. Not all of the thugs escaped.

Some—perhaps the slower ones, or those who foolishly tried to swat at a fairy—were caught. And in the hands of the fairies, justice was swift and slightly… decorative.

Strung up by enchanted vines, a handful of the brutes now dangled from high branches like hideous fruit, their muffled complaints echoing through the leaves as fairies flitted around them, occasionally poking at their noses or braiding their hair into elaborate humiliations.

Micah and Sniffles, now half-freed, sat blinking in the sudden quiet, watching as the last thug vanished with a scream that could shatter glass.

A fairy fluttered down and patted Micah on the nose.

Then winked.

The rabbit finished chewing through the final rope with a satisfied grunt and sat back, nose twitching.

Micah reached down, picked it up, and cradled it with all the reverence of someone who had just saved a cotton ball with teeth. "I knew you were special," he whispered.

Sniffles spat out his gag and wiped his mouth. "Micah. Your rabbit brought a fairy army."

Micah nodded.

"I always suspected he had connections."

Micah watched with wide eyes, hugging the rabbit close like a child clinging to his favorite stuffed toy.

"You're amazing," he whispered, booping its twitchy nose.

Scene: the grateful nymphs' blessing

The glade shimmered with an unearthly glow as the nymphs emerged from hiding, drifting across the moss like leaves on a breeze. Their laughter was like windchimes stirred by summer wind, sweet and strange, brushing against the skin and soul alike.

Micah blinked. "Are we... dreaming?"

One of the nymphs—taller than the rest, with golden bark twining through her hair—approached him and Sniffles, her eyes luminous as moonlight through mist. Without a word, she lifted a wreath woven from glowing forest leaves, cedar branches, and tiny blossoms that seemed to hum with gentle life. She crowned Micah, then Sniffles, with solemn grace.

The wreaths warmed against their skin—honey-sweet and cedar-rich, like summer rain and old, forgotten lullabies.

Sniffles touched his head gingerly. "Are we married now?"

"Shhh," Micah whispered, struck speechless by the sudden swell of calm. The leaves seemed to pulse faintly in time with his heartbeat.

The nymph bowed her head. "You defended our glade, the heart of the forest, when others fled. That memory will not rot like fallen wood. The forest remembers."

Micah looked around, now seeing the faint burn scars on the trunks behind the clearing—ghosts of an ancient fire. His chest tightened.

"Thank you, friends," he said quietly. "The forest remembers."

Behind them, another nymph stooped and pressed her fingers into the earth. Where she touched, a faint glow spread, reaching toward Micah's feet like a rootless blessing. "May this light guide you through darker realms," she said. "Jorg's Hold lies ahead. The forest can go no further."

The nymphs began to retreat, vanishing one by one into swirls of falling leaves.

Sniffles sniffed. "Well. That wasn't ominous at all."

Micah held the wreath steady on his head, gaze lifting toward the distant outline of the cursed mountain. "We're not alone," he said. "Not really."

Micah beamed.

Sniffles mumbled something about "allergic to gratitude," but wore the wreath anyway.

With their job complete and their egos significantly inflated, the duo set off toward the forest's edge.

The fairies—playful to the end—lit the path before them, creating a flickering tunnel of soft blue and gold. Their wings glowed like fireflies dipped in moonlight, illuminating the trail just enough to avoid more root-related accidents.

As the pair reached the final bend, Micah turned and waved to them.

"Thank you! Stay sparkly!"

A dozen tiny voices giggled in response. A fairy blew him a kiss. The rabbit, seated now on a mushroom throne like a visiting dignitary, gave a single solemn nod.

Then the forest faded behind them.

Back on the open road, Sniffles adjusted his pack and scratched under his wreath.

"Well, my friend," he said, brushing fairy glitter off his shoulder, "where to now?"

Micah tapped his chin thoughtfully. "Hey, remember that town called Beggar's Keep? It is not that far from here."

"Does it have ale?"

"Does it float in ale?"

Sniffles grinned.

 "Then that's the place for us. And we must find a bard to sing of our daring rescue! With fire! And wings! And a rabbit general commanding an army of glittery doom!"

"We'll just… leave out the part where we were tied up and gagged," Micah added quickly.

Sniffles nodded. "Obviously."

Rewriting history in their heads, they marched onward, puffed up with heroic pride and the heartfelt belief that they had masterminded the entire operation.

They skipped.

They boasted.

They accidentally walked into a ditch—but climbed back out with all the dignity of seasoned adventurers.

And so they made their way toward Beggars Keep—a quaint town with dubious morals, strong drinks, and, as fate would have it, a few problems of its own just waiting for two self-declared heroes to stumble upon them.

Beggars Keep.

A name that practically coughed when you said it.

Perched on the frayed hem of the kingdom of Noria, it was a place cobbled together from driftwood, regret, and desperation. The streets were crooked, the roofs slouched like old men, and the smell of low tide clung to the walls like a permanent ghost. But despite its ramshackle reputation, Beggars Keep was, oddly enough, a place of opportunity. It was a town of last chances, lost causes, and people who couldn't afford to be picky about the difference.

Micah and Sniffles shuffled in just as the sun dipped behind the sea-stained rooftops. Dusty, parched, and slightly glittery from leftover fairy dust, they made a beeline toward the only tavern in town—a charmingly rundown establishment with a swinging wooden sign that read: Watering Hole (though someone had crossed out "Hole" and scrawled "Mistake" beneath it in chalk).

Inside, it was loud. It was sticky. And it smelled like beer, brine, and deeply questionable life choices.

"Just like home sweet home," Sniffles muttered.

They squeezed their way through the packed room, dodging elbows and sloshing mugs. The only table with seats was already occupied by a very large, very unconscious, and very intoxicated minotaur.

He slouched in his seat like a collapsed tent, one horn skewed through the handle of his mug. He was mumbling into his ale-soaked beard about something vaguely resembling a valuable trinket and something else about being unfairly banned from a poker game involving a goat and a priest.

Micah and Sniffles exchanged a glance.

"Opportunity?" Micah mouthed.

Sniffles nodded slowly. "Opportunity."

They slipped into the seats opposite the minotaur, who remained blissfully unaware of their existence.

Micah leaned in as the massive creature burbled, "…precious trinket… couldn't keep it… too many eyes… map… no, wait, goats…"

Sniffles perked up.

"Did he say map?"

"I think he said goats."

Micah began rummaging through his robe pockets until he produced a crumpled, water-stained parchment—the same worthless map he'd lifted from the bottom of the supply closet back at the school. It had once been part of a failed cartography project—or possibly an elaborate prank.

Either way, it looked ancient and essential.

He discreetly showed it to Sniffles.

"Look," he whispered. "Old. Wrinkly. Sort of smells like wisdom. And see? A big 'X.' Classic treasure stuff."

"You're sure it's not the exit marker for the school latrines?"

Micah shrugged.

"Only one way to find out."

He cleared his throat dramatically and leaned toward the minotaur.

"Good evening, my horned friend," he said, extending a hopeful hand.

The minotaur blinked one eye open. There was drool involved. A lot of drool.

He stared at the offered hand.

Then at Micah.

Then at the ceiling.

Then back to his mug.

"Grhm," he said.

The hand was not shaken.

Sniffles jumped in quickly.

"We come bearing a proposition, sir," he said, trying to sound more like a merchant and less like someone who once bartered his boots for soup.

"A trade," Micah said helpfully, holding up the map with a flourish. "A very valuable treasure map in exchange for that, er, glittering item you were so eloquently describing."

Sniffles added, "Given your… remarkable strength and—uh—impressive horns, we figured you'd be just the adventurer to track it down."

Micah leaned closer, whispering, "Also, it might involve goats."

The minotaur's brow furrowed. He blinked at the map.

Then down at the small metal trinket hanging from a bit of leather at his belt, shaped like a minotaur, etched with strange symbols.

He grunted.

Unhooked the trinket.

And slammed it onto the table in a gesture of great importance, knocking over a bowl of peanuts and a sleeping mouse.

Then he took the map.

Unfolded it.

And squinted.

Then hiccuped.

Then, with all the dignity of someone making an excellent life decision, he nodded solemnly, handed them the trinket, and immediately fell face-first into his bowl of stew.

Micah snatched the trinket gleefully.

Sniffles pocketed the peanuts.

"Thank you, good sir. It was a pleasure doing business with you."

Micah gave a grand little bow, but the gesture was entirely unnecessary. The minotaur had already collapsed face-first into his stew with the sound of a cannonball hitting mashed potatoes. His massive frame hit the floor a moment later, snoring so loudly the tavern windows rattled.

Micah and Sniffles looked at each other.

Then at the trinket.

Then, without a word, they snatched it, scrambled from their seats, and bolted from The Watering Hole with all the grace of two squirrels fleeing a bakery.

They didn't stop running until they found a quiet barn on the edge of town, nestled beside a lopsided fence and a suspiciously watchful cow. The smell was familiar—hay, manure, and the faint trace of wet sheep—but it was safe. Safe-ish.

They tucked themselves into a dry corner behind a stack of hay bales, hearts still racing from their daring acquisition.

They might have slept straight through until morning if not for the ruckus outside.

Hooves clopped. Voices muttered. Something thudded. Micah blinked awake and nudged Sniffles.

"Did you hear that?"

The two crept to a small crack in the barn wall and peered out.

Down the lane, under the dim light of a flickering street lamp, four huge men were struggling to lift something even larger. With great effort, they heaved the unconscious minotaur into the back of a rickety wagon—his horns scraping the side, one foot twitching with residual snores.

"Is that…?"

"Yep," Sniffles said. "That's him."

"And they're…"

"Taking him home, I guess?"

One of the men muttered, "Next time he drinks that much, tie him to the dock instead."

The wagon creaked and clattered away down the road, the minotaur snoring like a tuba full of gravel. Micah and Sniffles exchanged a look. Then they lay back down, relieved.

"Well," Micah yawned, tucking the trinket under his arm, "that went better than expected."

"You say that now," Sniffles mumbled, already drifting back into sleep. "Wait till we find out what that trinket does."

Chapter Ten: Kaldir's Great Loss

(and Other Hangover-Related Mysteries)

"I can't believe I lost it!"

Kaldir stomped around his loft, nostrils flaring, hooves clomping angrily against the warped wooden floor. The room wasn't much—just a single space crammed above the village stables—but it was home. Or at least it smelled like one. Hay, sweat, and faintly roasted manure. Fortunately, the stench discouraged visitors. Or relationships. Or anything remotely resembling domestic peace.

He snatched up his worn leather shoulder bag and gave it a violent shake.

Thwunk.

A rock-hard piece of dried cheese thudded to the floor like it was angry, too.

Kaldir blinked. Then shrugged.

"Might be useful," he muttered, giving it a sniff and popping it back inside. "Y'never know when you'll get surrounded by feral mice."

He chuckled to himself—until the memory returned like a cold slap.

The trinket.

His brow furrowed. He dove back into the bag, rummaging through years of accumulated nonsense—old buttons, a cracked flute, something that may once have been a handkerchief but now resembled a crime scene—still no sign of the precious object.

Something thin and folded fluttered to the floor. He picked it up absently, stuffed it into his pocket without a glance, and kept searching.

"Where could I have—? The Watering Hole." His voice dropped to a groan.

Yes. That was it. It must have fallen out at the tavern last night.

Kaldir rubbed his temples as if massaging his memory might bring it back. He was a regular at the Hole—if only because no one else could drink as much as he could and still walk out (sometimes). Last night, they'd rolled out a new batch of dwarf spirits, and Kaldir, ever the noble volunteer, had appointed himself as chief taste tester. He'd done an excellent job. Or a terrible one. The details were… murky.

His stomach twisted. His head pounded. Somewhere behind his eyes, tiny dragons were hosting a very loud jousting tournament. And as for his tongue, it had glued itself to the roof of his mouth like an old shoe stuck in tar.

"I could drink a barrel of water," he rasped, smacking his lips.

Then, quieter, with genuine despair:

"How could I be so stupid?"

He slumped onto the edge of his rickety bed, cradling his pounding head in his hands. That trinket wasn't just valuable — it was important. More important than he'd ever let on. And now some idiot in that bar might have it. Or worse—sold it.

"No one better had touched it," he growled under his breath, his eyes flashing.

Kaldir hauled himself upright, grabbed his bag, and staggered toward the door, barely pausing to kick on his boots. The Watering Hole was about to get a very large, very hungover, and very irate minotaur at its doorstep.

Chapter Eleven: Suspicion, Sweat, and Strangers With Shifty Eyes

Climbing down the loft ladder with the grace of a boulder in free fall, Kaldir was instantly assaulted by the thick, eye-watering smell of dung. It clung to the walls. It haunted the air. It practically introduced itself. His hooves squelched faintly in straw, and as he turned toward the exit, he spotted a wide-eyed stable boy frozen in place, mouth ajar in dumbstruck awe.

To be fair, the boy had probably seen minotaurs before—but not like Kaldir. Not with his barrel-shaped gut slung proudly over his belt and thighs like overfed ham hocks, swaddled in old leathers and bad decisions. Truly, Kaldir was less warrior-poet and more beer barrel with horns.

The boy gawked.

Kaldir growled.

The boy bolted.

"Good," Kaldir muttered with a satisfied snort. "Let that be a lesson. Curry my favor and you might get the horns."

Out on the main path, the morning sun dared to exist, and his headache throbbed with every shaft of light that touched his skull. He trudged toward the Watering Hole, doing his best to avoid jarring his already dragon-drummed brain. Then, ahead of him, two figures caught his weary eye.

A small gnome, burdened with an oversized backpack that seemed to bounce in all directions, and beside him, a frazzled, pouch-covered human, likely a wizard, judging by the way he appeared at war with his staff. The wizard's robe swayed like it had too many secrets—and too many snack pockets. They were scurrying down the road towards him, darting glances at him, avoiding Kaldir's gaze with all the subtlety of two guilty raccoons.

As the gnome zipped past him, his pack grazed Kaldir's massive arm. The minotaur flinched—partly from the contact, mostly from reflex—and glared down, expecting at least a muttered apology.

Nothing.

The gnome sprinted ahead, head low, catching up to his wizard friend in a puff of dust and hurried footsteps. Kaldir narrowed his eyes.

"Tourists," he growled.

Annoying wanderers with nothing better to do than clog up roads with their hopeful dreams and jangly bits of junk. They probably thought they were adventurers. Most likely on some harebrained quest for a 'sacred muffin' or a 'lost sock of destiny.'

Still… something about them was familiar.

His foggy brain hiccupped on a thought.

They were at the Watering Hole. Last night. Sitting nearby. He clenched his fists as the pounding in his head briefly subsided, clarity peeking through like dawn through clouds. They had been there. They'd skittered around him earlier, same as now—no eye contact. No pleasantries. Just guilt, cloaked in dusty robes and gnomish shuffles.

"Suspicious little weasels."

He slowed his walk and turned, watching them hustle away. Their behavior was decidedly sketchy.

Kaldir stopped abruptly and turned, staring at the two travellers, a lightbulb going off in his muddled brain. Maybe they had his trinket!

He began to follow, picking up his pace, hooves crunching on gravel, hangover momentarily forgotten.

If those two miscreants had what was his... They wouldn't be able to outrun a hungover, determined, and slightly cheese-scented minotaur.

Not for long.

Chapter Twelve: The Reckoning of the Righteous—and Slightly Hungover

Kaldir kept his distance, close enough to overhear but far enough to avoid detection. His heavy hoof steps were muffled by the packed dirt road, and a sharper, more focused irritation was slowly replacing the dull throb in his head.

Ahead of him, the gnome—Sniffles, as it turned out—was giggling like a schoolboy who'd just sold someone a frog in a bottle labeled "Magical Elixir."

"Good thing we found that brute and his treasure to trade with!" Sniffles tittered. "That map was useless, but at least we can sell this trinket for lots of gold!"

Kaldir's left eye twitched.

"Poor sod," he grumbled under his breath. "I knew it. Swindled. Like a cow at a butcher's party."

He slowed slightly as the human, a wizard, or at least a man desperately trying to look like one, pulled something from one of his many bulging pockets.

It shimmered.

It gleamed. It was his trinket.

Kaldir froze.

"That's mine," he whispered.

Then, louder.

"THAT'S MINE!"

And just like that, Kaldir was charging.

Hooves thundered. Steam practically shot from his flared nostrils. His shaggy mane flew behind him like a war banner of sweat and misplaced dignity. His eyes were wild with rage, his horns gleaming dangerously in the rising sun.

Micah and Sniffles turned, faces contorting into matching expressions of horror. They didn't have time to run. In one breathless moment, they were lifted bodily into the air, and each gripped like an empty ale mug in one of Kaldir's massive fists.

"THAT'S MY TRINKET!" the minotaur bellowed, his voice making birds scatter from the trees and small mammals consider early hibernation.

Sniffles flailed, legs dangling like a marionette on his lunch break.

"Unhand us, you brute!" he squeaked, though his shirt cuff was currently wedged against his neck in a way that made speaking somewhat... squeakier than usual. Micah, meanwhile, was locked in a desperate internal monologue about how this would be a horrible time to miscast another spell. His feet wiggled in the air.

"I, I say," he said, trying for dignity and failing spectacularly. "How you've accosted us is barbaric! I have half a mind to report you to the constables!"

"Maybe only a quarter," Sniffles croaked. "You don't want to give it all away."

Micah blinked.

"Yes. A quarter. Thank you, wise as ever, Sniffles." He reached over and awkwardly patted Sniffles on the back. Sniffles nearly choked.

Kaldir, still holding them aloft, growled. "WHERE. IS. MY. TRINKET!!??"

Micah's eyes darted.

"You mean the one I just admired and maybe possibly accidentally acquired through what can only be described as enthusiastic bartering?"

Kaldir snorted. A blast of steam hit both of them square in the face.

Sniffles gagged. "By the gods, what do you EAT?!"

Kaldir shook them. Not roughly, just enough to rattle their bones and whatever marbles Micah had left rolling around upstairs.

"I'm going to give you two exactly five seconds to explain yourselves before I use one of you to stir the other's soup."

Chapter Thirteen: Technicalities, Tankards, and the Tipping Point

The Minotaur snorted and opened his fists, dropping Micah and Sniffles like sacks of old potatoes. They hit the ground with twin "oofs," tumbling into a tangle of limbs, robes, and dented pride. Groaning, they straightened themselves, brushing off dirt and dignity. Sniffles adjusted his satchel, while Micah attempted to smooth his hair with all the grace of someone who had never actually brushed it before.

Facing the towering Minotaur, Sniffles reached into his pack and produced the gleaming trinket. Holding it aloft like a relic of kings, he pointedly declared:

"Our trinket," he said, inching sideways to stay upwind of Kaldir's breath, which had the power of a moldy cheese wheel left too long in a swamp.

Kaldir blinked slowly.

"As of last evening, when you traded it for our map and another pitcher of ale," Sniffles continued, voice carefully neutral, "this fine artifact is—legally and morally—ours."

The Minotaur's brow furrowed.

"What are you nattering on about?" he rumbled. "The last thing I remember is wishing I had another tankard…"

Micah nodded encouragingly.

"Which we kindly provided you with—along with a historical map that may or may not lead to untold riches—in exchange for this," he gestured delicately at the trinket, "a very fair trade."

Kaldir crossed his arms. His muscles bulged.

"That deal was made when I was over-tired. You took advantage of my exhaustion. It shouldn't count."

Sniffles scoffed. "If by over-tired you mean spectacularly drunk, then yes. We did take advantage of that."

Micah's eyes widened.

"Ow!" Sniffles yelped as Micah jabbed him in the ribs.

"I mean—uh—oh crap," Sniffles muttered, realizing what he'd just confessed. His eyes darted back and forth like a trapped animal sizing up the exit route vs. death by hooves.

Micah, desperate now, cupped his hand and whispered into Sniffles' ear. The gnome frowned and tilted his head. Then, understanding dawned. He straightened up and cleared his throat with a diplomatic cough.

"My wise companion has come up with a solution we hope will settle this... confusion to everyone's satisfaction."

Kaldir's face was turning a shade of red usually reserved for volcanic eruptions and poorly cooked lobster. Encouraged by sheer self-preservation, Sniffles started speaking faster.

"You see, good sir," he said with a nervous smile, "what if instead of fighting about who owns what, we agree to share the artifact—and the map. As... co-owners. Adventuring partners!"

Micah threw his arms wide.

"Yes! Think of the possibilities. We follow the map—together—and split whatever riches we find. Three brave souls! Destiny! Brotherhood! Cooperative treasure-hunting!"

"And," Sniffles added, "we'll even let you name the group. Something cool. Like... The Horned Vanguard."

"Or," Micah said excitedly, "the Beef and the Brains!"

Kaldir looked at them both.

Hard.

Then at the trinket. Then, at his nearly empty coin pouch. Then back at them.

"…I'm thinking," he grumbled.

Kaldir frowned ferociously, and a low growl escaped his pursed lips. The gnome and the wizard were looking at him in terror, getting ready to make a run for it when Kaldir, already fed up and still very much hungover, not to mention intrigued with the thought of dwarf spirits for a year, said, "Fine, don't be hasty. I suppose you have a point about our deal, even if I don't recall it."

He glared with lowered brows at the pair of would-be adventurers. Reluctantly, and in much need of relaxation (the dragons were still jousting in his head), Kaldir agreed to listen to the pair.

That's when it happened. The trinket—still clutched tightly in Sniffles' hand—began to glow. Not a soft shimmer. Not a gentle hum.

A sharp, searing pulse of blue light surged outward with a crackling snap of static. All three leaped back—Sniffles yelping and flinging it into the dirt as if it had just whispered tax information into his brain. The trinket vibrated on the ground, glowing hotter and hotter, its carved runes flaring to life. Then—

BOOM.

A shockwave burst from it like a thunderclap, knocking them all flat on their backs. Birds scattered from nearby trees. A haystack a few yards away caught fire. A passing chicken keeled over, offended by the commotion.

Micah groaned from the grass. "I think I summoned something."

Sniffles sat up, dazed, and blinked. "I think it was my last meal."

Kaldir rolled over with a grunt, his mane sticking up in twenty directions. He looked toward the now-still trinket, which lay innocently in a small crater of scorched earth. And then, writing appeared. Glowing golden letters hovered above it, forming words none of them had seen before: "The bond is sealed. Seek the Hold. Five possible paths, one fate."

The light shimmered, then burned away into the air like smoke. The three stared at each other in stunned silence. Then Kaldir growled, pointing at the trinket.

"You broke it!"

Micah pointed right back. "You booby-trapped it!"

Sniffles flailed between them. "Maybe it's just... allergic to lying?"

The Minotaur snorted and picked up the still-warm trinket, now humming quietly in his palm.

"We're stuck together, aren't we?"

Micah nodded solemnly. Sniffles whimpered. Kaldir sighed.

"Fine." He looked at them both. "But if I die because one of you casts a spell using frog toes and elbow grease, I will haunt your bones."

Micah raised a hand. "Just to clarify, I usually know what ingredients I'm holding."

Sniffles groaned. "Oh, we are so doomed." *And what does five mean?*

Chapter Fourteen: Of Crowns, Coins, and Questionable Apples

The three companions arrived at The Watering Hole just as its battered door creaked open for business. The building sagged to one side as if it had given up on structural dignity years ago, its roof patched with mismatched shingles and one defiant cabbage leaf. Kaldir looked it over and snorted.

"Glad the dwarf spirits tell a better tale than the walls do," he said, already headed inside. "We need supplies. Here—" he handed over a pouch of clinking coins with the air of a general issuing war orders. "Get what we need for a few days' travel. I'll get us some mutton soup."

With that, he sauntered into the tavern without so much as a glance behind him. Micah watched him go, hands on his hips.

"Who named him ruler of all Noria? Shall we buy him a crown at the market?" he scoffed.

"Perhaps we can form him a crown out of horse dung—seems fitting," Micah grumbled.

"Come on, slave," Sniffles giggled, puffing out his chest dramatically." The master has spoken."

The two smirked and skipped around the corner like a pair of mischievous imps on holiday, leaving the towering Minotaur to his mutton soup and assuming authority. As they ambled down the winding path toward the market, the sea breeze was tousling Micah's robes and rustling Sniffles' absurdly large satchel; their conversation naturally turned to treasure.

"I hope this quest pans out," Micah sighed. "I'm tired of scrounging for half-stale biscuits and ale that tastes like goat regret."

Sniffles nodded sagely—and immediately buried a finger in his nose, digging like a miner with a grudge. Being a gnome, his nose was not so much a feature as a landscape. Micah had once likened it to a large yam with nostrils. Watching him excavate it was an experience he did not care to repeat. He picked up the pace.

"Let me know if you find the Lost Jewel of Andoral in there," he muttered, keeping a safe distance.

Rounding a bend, they reached the market square of Beggars Keep. The sun bounced off copper pots, fish scales, and one overly ambitious street performer attempting to juggle ferrets. Townsfolk bustled about— some with baskets of goods, others with shifty eyes and dirtier intentions. Pushing through the throng, they came to the first supply cart they saw.

It was manned by a grizzled human vendor who looked like he'd spent his life inhaling salt air and glaring at children. He spotted them instantly and made a low growling sound deep in his throat.

Micah froze mid-step. Sniffles' eyes darted. The man remembered them. More specifically, he remembered Sniffles from another market square—and the last time he'd tried to pick an elderly gentleman's pocket near this very cart.

Unfortunately, the gnome had misjudged the length of the chain on the old man's watch. Instead of nabbing the coin purse, he ended up tangled in the chain, dragged a good six feet before the chain snapped, and Sniffles scurried away like a startled ferret. Micah, of course, had been laughing too hard to help, nearly tumbling into a turnip display in the process.

To this day, they weren't sure what hurt worse—Sniffles' pride or the rock someone had hurled in their direction. Possibly both. Now, the vendor's eyes narrowed. Micah cleared his throat and approached with all the charm he could muster.

"Good day, sir! We require supplies." He smiled so wide it almost hurt. "For a very noble, respectable, definitely-real quest."

The vendor didn't blink.

"You'll get nothing until I see your coin. Be quick. I've got proper customers waiting."

Sniffles, undeterred, pulled a jingling pouch from his tunic and gave it a cheerful shake. The vendor's scowl cracked into a mercantile grin.

"Why didn't you say so?" He threw out his arms. "Welcome, fine gentlemen. Feast your eyes."

The vendor's sly smile widened as he swept his arms over his modest display of goods—half-stale bread, dried meat, cracked cheese wheels, and slightly wilted turnips arranged with a sort of defensive optimism.

Sniffles and Micah leaned in with exaggerated interest, haggling like seasoned adventurers, or, more accurately, like two desperate loafers trying to squeeze every copper's worth from their dwindling pouch. After a few grunts, eye-rolls, and one very dramatic eyebrow raise from Micah, they settled on a price.

As Micah counted the coins, Sniffles—ever the opportunist— spotted his moment. With sleight of hand that would impress even a street magician, he scooped up two apples and slid them under his shirt, quick as a blink.

Micah noticed, raised an impressed eyebrow, and gave his friend a subtle nod. The vendor, now suspicious of their sudden eagerness to leave, handed over their bundle of supplies, eying them both with the kind of look usually reserved for weasels at a henhouse gate.

"Odd little pair," he muttered, squinting after them as they made their hasty retreat.

Just as the market's energy reached its midday crescendo—vendors shouting, coins clinking, chickens clucking somewhere far too freely—disaster struck.

Sniffles paused mid-step. A look of horror crossed his face. That tickle. Micah turned slowly. "Oh no."

Sniffles' eyes widened. His nostrils flared. His entire gnomish body tensed like a trebuchet wound too tight.

"Sniffles—don't you do it—"

"Ahh… AH—CHHOOO!!!"

It was less a sneeze and more a compressed air explosion. A gust of hurricane-force wind erupted from his face, slicing through the air like a battering ram.

Micah's hat flew off his head, spiraling into the sky with the elegance of a frisbee hell-bent on reaching orbit. A nearby goose shrieked and flapped out of the way just in time. One unfortunate merchant's toupee was lifted clean off his scalp and caught midair by a startled child who immediately tried to wear it like a crown. The shockwave rattled market stalls, sending apples rolling and turning dry bread into shrapnel.

Micah stood frozen, hair sticking straight up, blinking slowly.

"…That," he said, brushing a turnip off his shoulder, "was majestic."

Sniffles wiped his nose, looking dazed but triumphant.

"Bless me."

The vendor, whose cart now resembled a poorly executed food sculpture, roared with fury. "THIEVES! WITCHCRAFT! DEVIANT SINUS SORCERY!"

Chapter Fourteen (Continued): Of Sneezes, Sprints, and Sprites

The merchant stood stiff as a plank, his nostrils flaring, his apple-strewn cart a battlefield of bruised fruit and broken dignity. Watching the two oddballs scamper off, he raised a fist to the sky with all the fury of a man whose day had been personally ruined by nasal artillery.

"I'll remember your faces!" he howled.

Then he sneezed once himself and muttered, "Blasted allergy season."

Around the corner, Micah and Sniffles kept running, completely unaware that their pursuer had already given up and gone back to inspecting his flying toupee.

They sprinted through town, knocking over a goat, startling a street mime (who broke character in a panic), and nearly bowling over a nun with suspiciously good reflexes. By the time they hit the outskirts of Beggars Keep, they collapsed in a tangled heap, panting like bellows in a blacksmith's forge.

"Did we lose him, do you think?" Micah gasped between gulps of air, one eye twitching involuntarily from the adrenaline.

Sniffles lay flat, arms out like he was making a dirt angel. He cocked one massive ear toward the underbrush.

And there it was.

A rustle.

Ominous. Mysterious. Possibly villainous.

Sniffles' eyes widened. "Rustle most foul!" he declared.

Then, in a flash of cowardice or cunning—no one could ever be sure—he shrieked, "Every man for themselves!"

And bolted.

A blur of gnome, he tore across the clearing like an acorn caught in a hurricane, leaving a whirlwind of leaves, dust, and panicked grunts in his wake. Micah, still on the ground, blinked.

"Traitor!" he shouted half-heartedly before dragging himself to his feet.

The bush rustled again. And out stepped......a twig.

Or at least, that's what it looked like at first—until it sneezed. A high-pitched, pollen-laced "Cheep!" echoed out, followed by a fluttering of tiny green leaves.

Then it spoke.

"Honestly. You'd think I was a bugbear the way you screamed."

Standing on the stump of a daisy was a two-foot-tall creature, gnarled of limb, leafy of the head, and grinning with the kind of mischief only a tree sprite could muster. He crossed his twiggy arms and tilted his leafy crown.

"Name's Twig. Been watching you two chaos goblins for hours. Top marks on the sneeze spell, by the way. Impressive air displacement for such tiny nostrils."

Micah stared wide-eyed.

"Did… did that shrub just compliment your sinuses?"

Twig puffed up with pride.

"Not just any shrub, thank you very much. I am Twig—guardian of glades, tickler of squirrels, and witness to your truly dreadful market etiquette."

Sniffles re-emerged from a bush, cheeks red.

"You're a… talking stick."

Twig narrowed his eyes.

"And you're a talking nose. Let's not cast twigs in glass houses."

Twig crossed his tiny arms—if you could call them arms, more like elegantly knotted twigs—and gave the two travelers a long, appraising look.

"You're lucky I intervened when I did," he sniffed, twitching a leafy eyebrow. "Another two minutes of that running, and one of you would've passed out from dramatic overexertion."

"I was conserving energy," Sniffles muttered defensively, brushing leaf bits off his tunic.

Micah nodded, still wide-eyed. "Also… I don't mean to question reality here, but why does a talking bush know about us?"

Twig huffed. "First of all, I am not a bush. I am a sprite—a guardian of the Lesser Glade, fourth circle of the Whispering Grove, distant cousin to the Mosslings of Fogmere, and once almost knighted by a squirrel."

He paused. "Long story. Involving acorns and minor theft. Irrelevant."

The two stared at him.

Micah whispered to Sniffles, "I think the shrub's lost its nut."

Twig grinned sharply. "Oh, I heard that, magic Misfire. And believe it or not, I came because that…" He pointed one knobbly finger directly at the trinket still clutched in Micah's hand, "Started glowing in the leyline beneath my roots. Woke me right out of my afternoon moss nap. And trust me, nothing messes with my nap unless it's cosmic."

Sniffles glanced at Micah. Micah looked at the trinket. The trinket shimmered faintly in response, pulsing with a quiet hum like a tuning fork set to destiny. Twig nodded, satisfied.

"Yep. You're on a stupidly dangerous quest. I'm coming."

Micah blinked. "Wait. You're joining us? Just like that?"

 "You need help," Twig said, leaping from the flower stump onto Sniffles' shoulder with the grace of a leaf on the wind. "You're hopeless in the wild, you angered a fruit vendor, and I heard one of you call the map a 'soggy napkin of destiny.'"

"That was me," Micah said proudly.

"Thought so." Twig clapped his barky hands together. "Right then. I'm your guide now. Congratulations—you've just been promoted from bumbling fools to bumbling fools with a tree consultant."

Sniffles sighed, but a smile tugged at his face. "I've had worse travel companions. One time, I journeyed with a ferret who stole my boots in my sleep."

"You wear boots?" Twig asked.

"I did once," Sniffles replied wistfully.

Micah grinned and pointed ahead. "To adventure then?"

Twig groaned. "Yes, yes. But do try not to sneeze us into another town this time."

Chapter Fifteen: Goats, Grog, and Gory Details

As fate would have it, Kaldir the Minotaur—formidable, imposing, and technically the "muscle" of the group—was the last thing Micah and Sniffles needed to worry about upon their return. The tavern had claimed him. More specifically, a particularly aggressive session of relaxation therapy involving three tankards of dwarf spirits (and a questionable fourth) had rendered him glassy-eyed and gloriously indifferent to anything not named "alcohol" or "entertainment."

He was currently lounging across two chairs, one leg propped on the third, gazing with the reverence of a man watching a religious miracle unfold. In front of him, a wiry street performer in an oversized hat balanced a pocket-sized goat on a barrel. The goat, dressed in a sparkly vest two sizes too small, was leaping through a miniature hoop with the finesse of a tipsy ballerina.

The crowd roared with laughter and clapped along in rhythm. Kaldir blinked slowly.

"'S a good goat," he mumbled, raising a toast that sloshed over the side of his mug and into his boot. "Besp' goat I ev—evah seen."

He didn't even flinch when Micah and Sniffles stumbled through the door looking like they'd been run through a hedgerow, rolled in moss, and sneezed out by a squirrel.

Micah's hat was askew, his robe had a suspicious stain on the hem, and Sniffles was clutching a crushed apple like a prized possession. Twig rode along tucked behind Micah's ear, arms crossed, smirking like he'd just watched someone walk into a beehive.

Whablazhapnedyo? Kaldir slurred, his words collapsing into each other like tipsy dominoes.

Micah opened his mouth, then closed it. Sniffles shrugged. Twig pointed dramatically at the trinket glowing in Micah's pouch.

"Destiny happened."

Kaldir squinted. "Dat goat jus' did a backflip."

The crowd whooped. Micah and Sniffles stood before Kaldir like two wet socks trying to pass as noble emissaries.

The Minotaur, leaning at a 45-degree angle that defied architecture, blinked slowly at them, his eyes glassy and unfocused, as though trying to read subtitles in a foreign film upside-down and underwater.

Whablazhapnedyo? he repeated, this time more of a murmur that ended in a hiccup and a victorious grunt.

Micah and Sniffles exchanged a glance that screamed, "This is our life now," and took a deep breath.

Sniffles, absolutely caked in mud and bad decisions, attempted a tone of elegance that his current appearance most definitely did not support.

"We, um… engaged in some… training exercises."

He paused. The silence that followed felt more accusatory than understanding. Even the pocket goat looked skeptical. Micah, lips twitching, gestured broadly to his disheveled robes.

"We were testing camouflage in adverse environments," he added.

From behind them, Twig gave a loud, dramatic yawn and called from his perch on a hanging lantern, "You ran from a fruit vendor and got ambushed by a moss puddle."

Sniffles shushed him with the urgency of a man being blackmailed by a shrub. Kaldir, now drifting sideways like a noble ship sinking in slow motion, gave a wise, vacant nod.

He stared at the performing goat, eyes glassing over in reverence.

"Goat knows… goat knows the truf."

Micah arched an eyebrow.

"The truth?"

Kaldir shook his head solemnly.

"Truuuuuf."

He attempted to lean back further and instead listed a full ten degrees to port, righting himself at the last second with the kind of sloppy grace exclusive to experienced drinkers and overfed cats. Micah couldn't help himself.

"Next time, perhaps we don't let our thief here plan the heist."

Sniffles, picking an unidentified twig from his sleeve, muttered,

"Hey, it worked... mostly."

Kaldir lifted his mug with the slow precision of a man performing delicate surgery on a liquid companion. Some of it sloshed onto the floor. Some of it splashed onto his leg. A heroic remainder made it to his lips.

He squinted at them, lifted the mug again, and slurred, "Nexsst time… you shtick wiff goats. Safers."

Twig, now lying belly-up on the lantern with his leafy feet dangling, let out a bark of laughter.

"And that's the wisdom of your warrior, ladies and gents. Follow the goat."

Chapter Sixteen: Stools, Stares, and Sudden Regrets

As the evening's chaos crescendoed—tankards clinking, laughter spilling from overstuffed tables, and the pocket goat bowing after a particularly dramatic pirouette—the front door of the Watering Hole slammed open with the theatrical flair of a low-budget villain reveal.

In waddled the merchant. His tiny eyes darted through the tavern like a hawk who'd misplaced his glasses and was now overcompensating with sheer personal vengeance. His apron was still stained with what could generously be called fruit residue, and tucked under one arm was an apple so bruised it looked like it had trauma flashbacks.

At a corner table, Micah and Sniffles froze mid-debate, halfway through arguing whether dragons needed deodorant or simply exhaled mint-scented destruction. Both gasped in unison.

"It's him," Micah hissed, dropping his apple core like a cursed relic.

"Operation Hide-Behind-the-Horns!" Sniffles declared, already ducking.

In a flurry of cloak, mud, and unearned guilt, the duo slid behind Kaldir, their oversized Minotaur companion, who sat still basking in a post-goat-show haze, humming vaguely along to a bard who couldn't keep time if it was strapped to his wrist. Now, a fundamental architectural truth must be mentioned:

Tavern stools are not made for Minotaurs. They creak. They wobble. They negotiate with gravity the way drunks negotiate with door handles.

As Micah and Sniffles crouched behind him like guilty shadows, they placed just enough pressure on Kaldir's stool to push it past the point of no return. The legs gave out with the sound of "SQUEEE-CRACK-THUD!"

Kaldir went down in slow-motion horror, a mug of dwarf spirits launching like a liquid cannonball into the air, splashing a bystander who immediately blamed it on the goat.

"By the tusks of Torvar!" Kaldir bellowed as he hit the ground like a falling wardrobe full of belligerence.

Everyone turned to look.

Everyone.

Including the merchant.

His eyes locked onto the tangled heap of Micah, Sniffles, a flailing Minotaur, and a startled Twig, who was now clinging to a candlestick with the expression of someone whose brunch had been interrupted by bandits. The merchant's face twisted into a rictus of glee, spite, and mild indigestion.

"YOU!" he bellowed, pointing a dramatically accusing finger at the pile. "Fruit-thieving, sneeze-blasting, goat-bothering little miscreants!"

Chapter Seventeen: The Face-Off That Wasn't

Kaldir's eyes—already red-rimmed from drink and dubious life decisions—narrowed to slits, like a pair of mischievous door hinges creaking shut on a burglar's fingers. His nostrils flared wide, snorting twin jets of fury and indigestion, a spectacle equal parts impressive and mildly alarming.

A hush fell over the tavern.

The merchant, mid-accusatory lunge, froze like someone who'd just realized they were standing in front of a very angry statue with hooves and a high alcohol tolerance. His finger wilted mid-air.

There was a pause.

A flicker of regret. And then, a deep, primal instinct—the fight-or-flight reflex of the typical coward—kicked in.

Faced with two options:

- Confront a hulking Minotaur currently rising like a mythical beast from the ruins of a broken stool, or
- Return home to his one-bedroom flat, lukewarm soup, and his judgmental cat, Mr. Whiskers— he made the only logical decision.

He spun on his heel so fast his apron nearly took flight, bumped into a chair, tripped slightly on a barmaid's mop bucket, and fled out the tavern door with the grace of a greased turnip tossed down a hillside.

In his wake, he left behind only:

- A fading trail of boot scuffs,
- A lingering stench of squashed apples and

- A few copper coins that may or may not have escaped his pocket in the panicked scrabble for the exit.

Kaldir, dusting himself off and righting the stool with one hand, sat back down with all the dignity of a slightly dented king returning to his throne.

"Didn't like his face," he said gruffly. "Too symmetrical."

Micah leaned in with a grin.

"Kaldir, my friend, you may have just saved our skins with nothing but a glare and a digestive snort."

"Minotaur magic," Kaldir mumbled, reaching for his untouched soup with a newfound sense of heroism.

Twig nodded solemnly.

"And thus, balance is restored: soup retained, apples defended, dignity… still in the red, but we'll call it a win."

Chapter Eighteen: Plots, Pickles, and Proper Planning

With a long, theatrical sigh that could've earned applause in more refined company, Galdon stared at the door through which the Grand Master had vanished.

"I would almost rather be back in the dungeon," he muttered, eyeing his mug of mystery brew with the same suspicion usually reserved for glowing mushrooms and tax collectors.

He took a reluctant sip, winced, and then decided it was only slightly better than moldy cell water. The tavern's raucous din began to thin as the night wore on, peeling away its drunkards, gamblers, and goat enthusiasts one by one. Galdon, ever the opportunist, drifted closer to the real prize—the odd trio in the corner: a gnome who gestured as if narrating a stage play, a human wizard with a cowlick that defied all magical logic, and a Minotaur whose contribution to the conversation mainly consisted of belches and burps of uncertain alignment.

Careful not to look like he was listening (though the Minotaur's lack of coherence made that easy), Galdon tilted his mug and his ear in equal measure. The name Jorg's Hold drifted faintly across the pub from the companions' table. The name lit up a dusty corner of his memory.

Jorg's hold

It was a mysterious, feared fortress shrouded in legend and deliberately erased from memory. Hidden in the mountains and surrounded by unnatural stillness, it's a place avoided by travelers and absent from maps. Elders speak of its haunted stones and eerie winds, warning that those who enter never return. Its origins are unknown, but one truth remains: it's a place best left untouched.

Perched on the jagged edge of the world, Jorg's Hold loomed like a forgotten god's last curse—a fortress carved into the bones of the mountain itself. Time clung to its stone walls like moss, thick and heavy, with towers that reached upward as if trying to escape whatever festered within. Black spires stabbed the sky, eternally rimmed with storm clouds that never drifted, as though the very weather had been chained in place. No maps dared mark its location. No birds flew near it. And no one who entered had ever returned—except for the occasional boot or whistle tumbling down the mountainside, which some optimists took as a good sign.

Whispers said the mountain itself was cursed, frozen in the exact moment of Jorg's fall—his betrayal, his final spell, and the sealing of a power so ancient, even time tiptoed around it. Runes flickered across the gates in a language older than fire, shifting and rearranging themselves whenever someone tried to read them. They said the air near the entrance was thick with something that wasn't quite mist and wasn't quite memory. It hummed, low and constant, like a warning that had forgotten what it was warning against.

Though none yet knew, the evil wizard, known only as the Grandmaster to those still living — who is also Micah's father — had once stood before its gate, power blazing around him like a bonfire in a snowstorm. But the hold rejected him. Magic of his magnitude curled and fizzled against the threshold like oil on water. He had roared, cursed the sky, and nearly shattered the mountain's face trying to force his way in. But the ancient enchantments held firm. Jorg's Hold would not open for the mighty. It had been built to keep out conquerors. And it did.

But fools? Fools could walk right in.

Galdon scratched his chin while a cold shiver ran up his spine like a ghostly finger.

"And here I thought this would be a simple fetch quest. These dolts are about to walk into a hornet's nest made entirely of rocks, rot, and regret."

He chuckled to himself, then groaned when he remembered he was going with them. "Less funny, that."

Still, he couldn't deny a certain thrill. He knew the route, knew the dangers. More importantly, he knew where to avoid actual work while still looking useful. A bard's true gift, after all, was presentation. He downed the rest of his drink with a grimace, tossed a copper on the table (though not his copper, of course), and climbed the crooked stairs to his assigned room—a bug-infested, mattress-shaped disgrace that smelled faintly of regret and pickled onions.

The morning after

Morning came much too soon and much too bright. Galdon awoke in the same position he had fallen asleep in: curled like a crab on the edge of the mattress, one sock missing, and a beetle sleeping comfortably in his beard.

"Lovely," he muttered, plucking it out and gently flicking it out the window. "Sleep well, my six-legged friend. You got the better bed."

He dressed quickly, adjusted his lute (which had one string left—hopefully the important one), and tiptoed down the stairs. The common room was now littered with passed-out patrons, limbs tangled like drunk marionettes. A snoring dwarf cradled a cabbage. Someone had drawn a mustache on the barkeep.

Chapter Nineteen: The Dawn of Dysfunction

What Galdon saw as he tiptoed back through the dim tavern froze him mid-step, his boot suspended mid-air like a bard's dramatic pause before the punchline. His eyebrows shot north, well past the normal bounds of facial expression, as he took in the scene before him—a sleeping arrangement so improbable, so artistically ridiculous, it demanded reverent silence and perhaps a sketch for future retelling in song form.

Kaldir, the hulking Minotaur, lay sprawled beneath the table like a particularly furry throw rug that had seen too many wash cycles. His one remaining boot pointed nobly to the heavens, the other nowhere in sight. His great belly rose and fell in rhythmic contentment, and he was snoring in slow, thunderous bursts—a natural percussion section in the orchestra of slumber.

Micah, ever the accidental opportunist, had curled beside him, nestled into the Minotaur's arm like it was a pillow gifted by fate and fur. His robes were half-askew, one sock dangling dramatically from a toe like a limp pennant, his fingers twitching with a half-finished dream-spell that might've summoned tea or a goat. But it was Sniffles, the gnome, who stole the entire theatrical production.

Perched regally on a chair, arms crossed and expression angelic, he had commandeered Kaldir's massive horns as makeshift footrests. His feet were propped up like a pampered prince, and he wore the kind of smile that suggested dreams of foot massages, bottomless pudding bowls, and jewel-encrusted everything. And then there was Twig.

Balanced precariously atop a hanging chandelier, the tiny sprite snored in soft hiccups, a half-eaten sugar cube clutched to his chest like a teddy bear. His wings drooped over the side like soggy curtains, and a faint glow pulsed with every snore, casting delicate sparkles over the chaos below. A hastily scribbled sign dangled from the chandelier by a bit of twine, clearly written in Sniffles' hand:

"Do Not Disturb. Sacred Sleep Ritual. Violators Will Be Hexed and/or Hugged."

Galdon stood there, utterly struck dumb by the beauty of the disaster. He exhaled slowly, set down his empty tankard, and whispered to himself,

"…I have got to write this down."

Galdon stood there, utterly struck dumb by the beauty of the chaos.

"This," he whispered to no one in particular, "is why I keep a journal."

He imagined the tale years from now, exaggerated for the stage. "Behold, the gnome who dared treat a Minotaur's horns like an ottoman, and lived to sigh contentedly about it."

The trio, unconscious but utterly choreographed, looked as though some cosmic playwright had staged them for maximum comedic resonance. A scene born not of strategy or bonding, but sheer exhaustion and misaligned gravity. Galdon gave a long-suffering sigh, equal parts exasperated and enchanted. This crew was a walking disaster... but by the gods, they were original.

Slipping through the tavern door and into the soft glow of early morning, he paused only to glance back once, tucking the image away like a treasured page in a much funnier story than he'd expected to live.

The door clicked shut behind him. And somewhere behind it, a Minotaur snored, a gnome dreamed, and a wizard muttered something about flying badgers.

Outside, the market was just yawning awake, stalls groaning under the weight of fresh bread, slightly wilted herbs, and the village's finest approximation of cheese. Galdon browsed quickly, picking up just enough travel food to appear responsible without threatening to actually be helpful.

"They'll be late," he reasoned, eyeing the rising sun. "That Minotaur had enough dwarf spirits to knock out a small bear."

His plan was simple: get ahead, look heroic, and absolutely avoid singing unless bribed. The less time he spent in earshot of judgmental fairies or angry squirrels, the better.

With a final check of his lopsided pack and a silent vow to absolutely not get attached to anyone in this absurd quest, Galdon set out toward the road leading north, toward Jorg's Hold, toward danger, and toward a payday he wasn't entirely sure existed. But then again, a little misdirection, a little performance, and maybe he'd come out on top after all.

Chapter Twenty: Late to the Luncheon, Just in Time for Trouble

It took much longer than anticipated for Galdon to procure the necessary camping and foraging supplies for the journey. The marketplace, bustling with midday bartering and the odd street performer juggling turnips, had not been kind to his wallet—or what remained of the wizard's coin purse.

"Stale bread, weevil flour, and something claiming to be dried jerky," he muttered, surveying his purchases with disdain. "Excellent. A banquet fit for a disgraced bard and his dubious fellowship."

The purse had proven insultingly thin, and the vendors of Beggars Keep were as charming as toothless wolves, giving no quarter to a man in need of credit. Galdon had tried his best to haggle, using his most dramatic storytelling voice to extol the nobility of their quest. Still, the only response he'd gotten was a turnip thrown with suspicious accuracy. By the time he returned to the Watering Hole, the place was already buzzing with the lunch crowd, thick with smoke, sweat, and the scent of questionable stew.

He swept the tavern with a practiced eye, but the trio of misfits—Minotaur, gnome, and chaos wizard—were nowhere to be seen.

"Great," he grumbled, adjusting the sack on his back and sighing so deeply it might've dislodged a pigeon from the roof.

Galdon pushed out into the streets again, scanning the thinning crowd. "No singing goat. No nasal gnome. No walking wardrobe with hooves." He quickened his pace, threading through vendors and wagons, elbowing past a man trying to sell enchanted spittoons, until finally, up ahead—

There.

Just beyond the city gate, striding into the dusty road that wound toward the hills, were his targets.

The Minotaur walked like someone recovering from a minor earthquake. The gnome bounced ahead, already chasing a bug with an impressive glint. The wizard—hood askew and staff tapping out the rhythm of distraction—was whistling a tune that may or may not have been from the frog-rain incident.

Chapter Twenty One: Of Hangovers and Horn-Based Innovation

The wizard and the gnome trudged onward like two poorly balanced barrels rolling uphill—pale, queasy, and full of regret. Micah's cheeks were greenish, and his staff tapped limply against the dirt like it, too, was hungover. Now and then, he muttered something about "never again... unless it's on a holiday."

But Kaldir—oh, Kaldir—was in a class all his own.

The massive Minotaur shuffled forward with all the grace of a collapsing barn, his head drooped so low his horns nearly touched the road. The twin spikes cut furrows in the dust, unintentionally inventing what would later be known in local farming circles as "minotaur plowing." Every few minutes, Kaldir would clutch his temples, the fur on his brow damp with existential despair. He'd emit a long, haunted groan that echoed through the trees like a foghorn played in a minor key.

"Why do the spirits betray me so?" he muttered.

Then, a pause.

"Wait, no. I betrayed them first. Never mind."

Trailing them from a discreet distance, Galdon kept pace with the cautious rhythm of someone who very much did not want to be noticed, especially by a wizard with unpredictable fingers, a gnome with questionable moral instincts, or a half-blind Minotaur who could snap him in half while reaching for a waterskin. Overhead, Twig floated in slow zigzags, flopping from one leaf to another like a paper lantern after a particularly emotional festival. He was also wearing someone's sock as a cloak—a gnome-sized sock, judging by the faint scent of sugared turnips.

"Oh dear," Twig sighed dramatically, shielding his eyes as if the sight of the hungover march was too much for his delicate nature. "The heroes of legend, ladies and moss-folk. Striding bravely toward destiny. Or perhaps just toward a bush they can throw up behind."

He landed briefly on Micah's shoulder. "You smell like fermented beet juice and shame."

"I feel like fermented beet juice and shame," Micah replied without looking up.

Twig fluttered off again, this time landing on Kaldir's horn and shouting down it like a megaphone: "Oi! Do the road a favor and lift your head, you're making ruts!"

Kaldir growled low in response, which made Twig grin and flap away just out of horn-swipe range. Somewhere behind them, Sniffles was singing an off-key ditty about sausages and poor life choices. And Galdon, wisely, kept to the shadows—humming to himself and pretending he didn't know any of them. He wasn't trying to eavesdrop. He simply had ears, and the trio made as much subtlety as a tavern brawl in a flute shop. And then he saw it.

The wizard — may the gods help him—glanced at Kaldir's drooping horns with an expression that rode the knife's edge between brilliant invention and pure lunacy.

His eyes widened. His lips parted in a giddy grin. His little fingers twitched like a tinkerer finding spare parts. Galdon slowed his pace, brows climbing, unsure whether to be intrigued, horrified, or ready to run.

Chapter Twenty Two: Horns, Hints, and Heightened Regret

The party had only made it a few miles beyond the city before the sun turned judgmental and the dust grew personal. As they trudged onward in mismatched rhythm—Minotaur groaning, wizard mumbling, gnome plotting—it became clear that spirits, sleep, and dignity had all been in short supply.

Then, as if scripted by the gods of awkward timing, Micah piped up.

"Hey, Kaldir," he said with that specific brand of gnomish innocence that often precedes suggestions better left unspoken. "My pack's feeling a bit hefty today, and you've got those, uh, strong horns, right? If you're going to walk with your head that low anyway, mind if I just hang it off one for a bit? Just until the next hill?"

The Minotaur emitted a sound that defied natural classification. Somewhere between a growl, a groan, and the low, tortured whimper of a bear forced to attend a mandatory etiquette seminar, the sound rumbled through the ground, causing a nearby squirrel to drop its acorn in alarm. Kaldir slowly turned his massive head, eyes glowing red with a combination of hangover, rage, and existential regret. His gaze locked with the wizard, a searing glare so potent it could curdle cream, dry up rivers, and convince the dead to stay dead. Micah's face froze.

There was a pause. Then came a cough—light, awkward, and entirely choreographed.

"No worries," the wizard amended, backpedaling with the grace of a bard caught lip-syncing. "I just realized I've been neglecting my... personal fitness goals. Ha! Silly me. I can lug my pack like the proud beast of burden I am. No need to, uh, inconvenience you with my gravity woes."

Galdon, still trailing at a reasonable distance to preserve his sense of independence and survival, covered his mouth to stifle a snort. The Minotaur resumed his dragging gait, rumbling under his breath about "dangling wizard ornaments" and "the fragility of peace."

Chapter Twenty Three: The Art of Observation (and Tumbling Gnomes)

Galdon kept his distance, shadowing the quirky trio like a reluctant chaperone to the worst field trip in history. With every mile, his amusement grew. He had not expected entertainment—he had expected incompetence, indeed, perhaps even doom. But this? This was a traveling sideshow masquerading as an adventuring party.

At mid-morning, the wizard—Micah, a name Galdon had only recently committed to memory after hearing it shouted repeatedly in exasperation—bent to examine a rock, presumably out of scholarly interest. Or maybe because it looked shiny. Either way, in one fluid and entirely unintentional flourish, Micah's staff swung sideways, executing a perfect low-sweep trip wire maneuver.

Sniffles, mid-step, had no chance. The gnome went airborne, arms flailing like a windmill on fire. He struck the ground with a thud, performed a forward roll that resembled a reluctant cinnamon roll uncoiling, and landed face-first in a bush. The bush, a thorny variety named Regretus Itchious, was not forgiving.

Galdon, watching from the tree line, nearly choked on a berry he'd been chewing. "Oh, gods," he whispered, wiping a tear. "They're alive entirely by accident."

But the day's highlight arrived after lunch. An errant breeze, sent no doubt by the universe's Department of Irony, whisked Micah's floppy wizard hat off his head and into the open sky. What followed could only be described as performance art.

The hat—animated, spirited, possessed by the very soul of freedom itself—danced and darted across the hills like a puckish fae creature. It vaulted over fences, skated along fence posts, and teetered precariously on the edge of a cow, which seemed mildly offended by the intrusion.

Micah gave chase like a man possessed, staff clutched in one hand, his other outstretched like a dramatic mime lost in a windstorm. Sniffles joined the fray, trying to assist, which only resulted in a series of gnomish acrobatics that defied physics and good taste. At one point, he attempted to leap from a stump to snag the hat mid-flight, only to be launched backward by a low-hanging branch with all the subtlety of a battering ram.

The entire ordeal lasted thirty-seven minutes. When at last the hat surrendered, fluttering gently into Micah's waiting hands as if to say, *Very well, mortal, you have earned me*, the wizard sank to his knees in triumph.

Sniffles collapsed next to him, gasping, "I haven't run that hard since I stole that turkey drumstick in Fumblegrove." Behind a thicket, Galdon leaned against a tree, shaking with laughter.

"The gods send me this lot," he murmured. "If a bandit doesn't kill them, they'll be eaten by a misplaced picnic."

But even as he laughed, something inside him shifted—a tiny flicker of something dangerously close to fondness. Not trust. Never trust. But…curiosity. These fools were heading toward Jorg's Hold, a place cloaked in shadow and legend. And somehow, these absolute disasters might just make it there—if only to set it on fire by accident.

Chapter Twenty Four: Camp, Commands, and Culinary Skies

By the time the sun began its theatrical descent, the sky igniting in a glorious smear of culinary colors—peach, mango, and a hint of burnt sugar—the weary travelers reached the threshold of the great forest. Trees loomed like ancient sentinels, whispering secrets to the breeze, and the air shifted—cooler, expectant.

Kaldir, deciding that his burdens had defied gravity, patience, and physics for long enough, dropped his pack with the grace of a collapsing bookshelf.

"Okay," he declared, in a tone carved from the same stone they used to make temple commandments, "we make camp here. Early start tomorrow."

He didn't ask. He announced. He then turned to the others with a gaze so intense it could strip wallpaper off a stone wall, his bloodshot eyes still glowing faintly, like someone who had stared into a dwarf spirit and seen his regrets staring back.

"Go gather wood."

There was a pause. A long one.

Then…

"Hey!" Sniffles piped up, his voice full of plucky gnomish indignation. "Who put you in charge?"

Micah nodded vigorously, clearly enjoying the rare sensation of righteous rebellion. "Yeah! There's two of us, and this was our idea. We're practically the founding fathers of this expedition."

Kaldir turned toward them with the slow deliberation of a guillotine being raised. His expression didn't change, exactly—it just tightened. A subtle shift. Like tectonic plates. The look he gave them was a seismic deterrent. It said: "I may not have claws, but I have hooves, muscle memory, and very little patience. I could flatten both of you into festival pancakes and still have time to toast them."

Micah and Sniffles both blinked. Then turned. Then scurried. Not with terror, no—with enthusiasm. *Yes. Let's go with that.* They marched toward the treeline with the purposeful stride of men who had absolutely not just been cowed into obedience by a hungover Minotaur.

As their silhouettes disappeared into the twilight, their voices continued—less bold now, more petty.

"I'm just saying," Sniffles muttered, "we outnumber him."

"Sure," Micah said. "But he outweighs us."

"And probably out-headbutts us, too."

They vanished into the forest, the shadows swallowing them as night began to bloom above, full of stars, sparks, and the sound of whatever weird thing was undoubtedly about to happen.

Back at the camp, Kaldir stretched out with a grunt, adjusted a rock into what could generously be called a pillow, and muttered, "Gnomes and wizards. Might as well travel with two confused squirrels."

Chapter Twenty Five: Of Beans, Nightmares, and Bushes That Judge Silently

From the edge of the clearing, Galdon squatted behind a large bush, resigned to his fate as the unofficial fifth wheel of a wagon that hadn't realized it was a cart yet. The bush wasn't exceptionally comfortable—it had opinions about intruders—and made those opinions known through an impressive number of twigs in sensitive places. Still, it offered just enough cover to observe the group without being noticed. Or so he thought.

High above, Twig floated lazily on a breeze, pretending to be absorbed in the delicate art of balancing a stick on his nose. But as his path looped over the clearing, his bright eyes flicked briefly toward the bush. He paused, just for a heartbeat. Then his wings beat once, and he hovered for a moment—head cocked, as if listening to some frequency no one else could hear. A knowing grin played at the corners of his tiny mouth.

With a faint, almost imperceptible nod in Galdon's direction, Twig twirled midair, somersaulted just to show off, and zipped back toward the group. He said nothing. Micah continued mumbling to his staff about the meaning of life and fermented root vegetables. Sniffles was arguing with a pinecone that may or may not have stolen his sandwich. Kaldir muttered something about honor and betrayal between bouts of melodramatic groaning.

And Twig? Twig just hummed softly to himself as he perched on Micah's hood like a decorative moth, looking for all the world like he hadn't noticed anything at all.

But he had. He always did. The Minotaur, ever the reluctant leader, had a roaring fire going in minutes, thanks to the surprisingly effective teamwork of his pint-sized companions. Once flames crackled and shadows danced, Sniffles produced a small pot and began a culinary process that could only be generously called soup.

The meal consisted mainly of rehydrated onions, some dried beans, and a hint of hope. Micah had offered to help by trying to "heat the pot magically," but after last time (when the beans achieved sentience and attempted to unionize), Sniffles waved him off with a firm "Go sit down and hum or something."

Micah did. And hummed. Softly. Aimlessly. Like a kettle about to boil but not quite committed to the idea.

As darkness folded around the clearing, Kaldir rolled onto his side with a grunt, using his pack for a pillow and a flat rock for lumbar support. He closed his eyes to the gnome's gentle hum, the fire's soft crackle, and the distant whisper of the forest. And then the humming shifted. It morphed.

In Kaldir's dreams, it transfigured into the dread tones of a dwarf bard—bearded, smug, and wildly off-key, plucking a lute as if it owed him money. The song? Something about goats and vengeance, sung in a pitch that violated treaties. The bard dissolved into two angry cats, screeching and swiping at each other with bloodcurdling yowls over a dead mouse that probably deserved better.

Kaldir, tangled in his blanket, snorted once, mumbled "By the hooves of the heavens…", and twisted onto his other side.

Eventually, the nightmare faded, and he slipped into a merciful, deeper sleep, the cats replaced by more soothing imagery—perhaps ale fountains, or horn-polishing maidens, or a world without singing dwarves.

Dawn arrived with its usual flair, splashing gold across the treetops. The fire was now embers, and dew clung to every blade of grass like glitter from the heavens.

Kaldir stirred, blinked once, and groaned. Then paused. No headache. He sat up slowly. No splitting pain. No pounding drums. No vengeful dwarven choirs in his skull.

"I feel… amazing," he said aloud, marveling at this alien wellness sensation. "I could almost go for some Dwarf brew. Shame we're out…" he added wistfully.

The gnome and the wizard were sleeping head to toe, using a ground sheet for a blanket and sharing it for warmth. With each breath, the gnome was snoring merrily, inhaling three inches of the wizard's sock into one of his oversized nostrils. The wizard was cuddling the gnome's big feet with a gentle smile. Kaldir gave a low chuckle.

The sound was soft, rare. Almost fond. And behind a bush just a few yards away, Galdon, wide awake and eating dried meat with unspoken judgment, muttered, "If this isn't the oddest band of halfwits I've ever shadowed…"

He popped a berry into his mouth, still not entirely sure whether to laugh, pity them, or quietly rescue them when they inevitably wandered into a goblin latrine.

Chapter Twenty Six: Of Beans, Boasts, and Bruised Gnomes

"Let's go!" Kaldir bellowed, chest puffed like a disgruntled forge bellows. "The sooner we get started, the sooner we're done. I'll finish this misbegotten 'adventure,' return to my clan, and spit on their boots."

He paused. "…Preferably after drinking a skin of dwarf spirits. Twice."

Grumbling, Micah and Sniffles shuffled to their feet, brushing leaves—and in Sniffles' case, a remarkably clingy beetle—off their cloaks. The wizard scraped the last of the congealed bean paste from the pot with the determination of a man who'd once tried to turn a mud pie into dinner. It wasn't great then either.

Trailing behind the hulking Minotaur like mismatched ducklings, they trudged into the woods. As the sun bled lazily behind the treetops, firelight sprang to life in their newest makeshift camp. Shadows danced and stretched, flickering across the gnarled roots and weary travelers.

Naturally, as stomachs filled (relatively speaking), a time-honored tradition began to emerge among the group: storytelling—that noble sport of embellishment, exaggeration, and outright fiction.

"—and that's how I got out of the dragon's nest," Micah declared proudly, swirling his hands like he was casting some kind of storytelling spell.

Sniffles snorted. "Sure. And I suppose next you'll tell me you single-handedly saved an elven kingdom?"

"I did," Micah said, eyes gleaming. "I've got the bow to prove it!"

"From where? A child's archery set?" Sniffles shot back, his nose twitching in amusement.

They argued louder, the crackling fire a Greek chorus to their escalating nonsense. Arms flew, voices rose, egos swelled. A stick waved through the air, possibly meant to be a spear. Someone used a frying pan as a helmet. And then— Thud. Whoosh. Whump.

Sniffles, mid-gesture describing a headhunter's ceremonial dance, caught a wayward shove from Micah. Time slowed. The gnome's expression turned from dramatic bravado to pure betrayal.

Chapter Twenty Seven: The Bush, The Britches, and The Bystanders

Down Sniffles went—arms flailing like a windmill possessed—into the thorny Toad Bush, a botanical nightmare infamous among forest-dwellers for being both unwelcoming and unapologetically inhabited. As Sniffles disappeared into its thorns, the bush let out a faint, almost gleeful squelch. It was, after all, not the gnome's first visit from the world of slapstick justice.

From within the foliage came a series of undignified sounds:

"OW!"

"Something licked me!"

"WHY IS IT STICKY?!"

Micah, face pale as parchment and expression contorted with guilt and panic, began hopping from foot to foot. "I didn't mean it! I didn't mean it!" he wailed, flapping his arms like a wizard trying to reverse time through interpretive dance. "I was gesturing, not shoving! There's a difference! One's expressive, the other's litigious!"

He turned toward the trees, casting his voice like a desperate spell: "Kaldir! Emergency! Gnome down! I repeat, gnome down!"

A thunderous crashing heralded the arrival of Kaldir, the Minotaur, whose footsteps sounded like someone dragging furniture through a gravel pit. He burst through the underbrush like an avalanche with opinions, branches snapping in protest as he bulldozed his way into the clearing. Skidding to a halt in a cloud of twigs and righteous indignation, he snorted once, stomped twice, and scanned the group with eyes full of purpose and slight confusion.

From the deep fold of his side pocket, a tiny voice piped up: "Smooth as ever. Subtlety is dead, and you're its horned executor." Twig popped his head out, blinking against the sunlight and brushing a leaf from his hair like a passenger disembarking from a particularly bumpy wagon ride.

He pulled himself up onto the pocket's edge like a prince on a parade float and added, "Next time, a warning before the death gallop, please. My spleen just tried to switch teams."

The sight that met him nearly knocked the rest of the ale from his system. There, upside down in the throes of shrubbery doom, hung Sniffles—legs akimbo, a constellation of thorns crowning his backside like the world's most awkward halo. His pants had migrated south, making an unscheduled departure from duty, revealing a full moon that shone defiantly beneath the forest canopy.

The gnome's rope belt hung in tatters—ribbons of defeat fluttering mournfully in the breeze, as if waving goodbye to the last shreds of his dignity.

Kaldir stared. Micah sniffled. Sniffles whimpered.

From somewhere deep in the bush came the ominous sound of a toad hissing. Kaldir cleared his throat and, very solemnly, declared, "Well. That's... a lot of gnome."

Then, because fate is cruel and dignity is optional, Twig the sprite popped out of Kaldir's pocket, hovering just overhead, eyes wide with delight and mischief. "Oh wow! That's not how you dive into a thistle bush," he chirped. "But I give it a 9 for form, and a solid 10 for comedy!"

The Minotaur exhaled slowly. "I'm going to regret this," he muttered, and trudged forward with all the enthusiasm of a man retrieving laundry from a very angry badger.

Chapter Twenty Eight: Twig's Trustworthy Toad Bush Rescue

Kaldir had just begun untangling Sniffles' leg from a particularly ambitious thorn when a blur of glitter and humming energy zipped between his horns.

"Stand back, everyone!" Twig announced, hands on his tiny hips, wings buzzing like a caffeinated dragonfly. "Fear not! For I, Twig the Magnificent, Master of Mirth and Minor Miracles, shall liberate the gnome!"

Kaldir froze mid-growl. "You what?"

"I've been waiting for my moment to shine!" Twig puffed out his chest, which, for scale, was roughly the size of a walnut.

Sniffles, hanging upside down and still pantless, mumbled from the depths of the thorny toad bush, "I swear, if I come out of this glowing or green…"

Micah clutched his staff. "Twig, maybe we should—"

But it was too late.

Twig was already mid-chant.

"By the power of petal and puff,

Free this gnome from scratchy stuff!

Unbind his limbs, release his pants,

And please don't summon any—"

POOF!

A thunderous burst of sparkles exploded around the bush, momentarily turning everything, including Kaldir, bright pink. Micah shielded his eyes. Kaldir blinked in disbelief, now radiating an unfortunate shade of cotton candy. Even the tree behind him glowed faintly with a rose-tinted blush.

The bush... shuddered. Then burped. And then, as if offended by the entire ordeal, it spat Sniffles out with a soggy splort, sending him tumbling end over end into Micah, knocking them both into a puddle with a unified squawk.

Sniffles sat up, dazed, pants now miraculously tangled around his neck like a scarf. "Twig," he said with a trembling voice, "what… did you do?"

Twig fluttered down, brushing his hands dramatically. "You're welcome."

"You turned the Minotaur into a marshmallow," Micah groaned, spitting out a leaf.

Kaldir stared at his hooves. "They sparkle."

There was a long, collective silence.

Twig just beamed. "That went much better than my last rescue! That time, the goat exploded."

Chapter Twenty Nine: Of Spirits and Strategy

As the wizard continued his dramatic sobbing, clutching his friend's scraped-up gnomish limbs like a nursemaid on the edge, Kaldir stood beside them with arms crossed and a face carved from granite—pink, sparkly granite, thanks to Twig's earlier "help."

"I just—hic—I didn't mean for the bush to fight back!" Micah sniffled. "It's all my fault! Look at him—"He's got bark in places bark should never be—in the most wildly inappropriate spots."

Sniffles, still recovering from his leafy reintroduction to gravity and humility, lay bundled in a tattered cloak, face down in the dirt, muttering things like "why does moss itch?" and "no, grandma, I don't want more soup."

Entered Galdon.

The dwarf approached carefully, hands raised in peace, his beard braided for maximum charm and utility. "Maybe I can help," he said smoothly, slipping into character like a bard slipping into a tale. "Those thorn scratches look fairly deep. You need something to disinfect them."

Micah shrieked—an alarmed yelp that came from somewhere near his pancreas—and wheeled around, eyes red-rimmed and face tear-slicked.

Kaldir, who had been glaring at the horizon with the patience of a storm, turned slowly. "We don't take kindly to—"

GLORRK. His voice caught in his throat because Galdon was holding out not one but two skins of dwarf spirits.

The first skin was offered with reverence. "For the wounds, of course."

The second? Ah, the second was held like a sacred offering. "And this… for those with more refined palates. You, my friend, look like a thirsty man."

Kaldir's eyes widened. His ears twitched. His hooves took a step closer without his brain's permission. The gnome and the wizard looked up, equally wary.

"I don't know…" Micah began, his moral compass poking its head above the tears. "You just appear out of nowhere? That's convenient, and I'm not—"

The Minotaur turned. Glared. Snorted. The force of the exhale blew out Twig, who had been hovering unnoticed behind Micah's ear.

Micah squeaked and folded like a napkin. "Welcome to the group!" he chirped. "I love strangers. Strangers are wonderful. Especially strangers with spirits."

Sniffles raised a thumb from his dirt nest and whispered, "Bring soup next time." Galdon bowed with a flourish, inwardly smug. Step one, complete. Befriend the buffoons. Now, let's see what this trinket is all about…

Chapter Thirty: Bonds and Bandages

Kaldir, having dutifully poured dwarf spirits over Sniffles' scratches—while humming what sounded suspiciously like a tavern drinking chant—leaned back on his elbows with a grunt of satisfaction. The second skin of spirits, now safely tucked into his belt pouch, sloshed a lullaby he fully intended to fall asleep to.

Sniffles lay facedown on a flat patch of moss, still occasionally twitching from phantom thorns. "I swear," he mumbled into the ground, "those bushes had a personal vendetta. And I still think I saw one smile."

"Perhaps they were enchanted?" Micah suggested cheerfully, poking the fire with his staff and sending a small cascade of sparks skyward. "Maybe part of an ancient dryad defense system. Or maybe… the toad bush is sentient!"

"Sentient or sadistic," Sniffles muttered. "Either way, it's got my backside."

"Bravely won," Galdon chimed in, settling in near the flames with practiced ease. "Every scar tells a story. Yours may scream it, but still."

Micah giggled and nudged Sniffles' shoulder with the end of his staff. "You should name them! All the scratches. That way, they feel appreciated."

Sniffles groaned. "Only if I get to name one Micah the Menace and another Kaldir's Idea of First Aid."

Kaldir let out a low, satisfied grunt. "I did my part. You're alive. You're patched. You didn't even faint." He paused. "Barely."

"I was going to faint artistically," Sniffles countered, propping his chin on his arms. "But then I remembered my dignity."

Micah nodded solemnly. "Which ran screaming into the woods about two hours ago."

Sniffles lifted his head just enough to glare. "You better not snore, Bard. My pain has granted me super hearing."

"Oh, don't worry," Micah said, eyes twinkling. "If he snores, I'll cast 'Featherfall' on your pillow—so it'll drift slowly over his face."

Kaldir snorted.

There was a silence, broken only by the crackle of the fire and one unfortunate fart from Kaldir, who offered no apology.

Chapter Thirty One: The Spirits of Brotherhood (and Bad Decisions)

As the second skin of dwarf spirits grew lighter, Kaldir's roars of laughter grew louder—and his personal space grew smaller. He slapped Galdon on the back with increasing vigor, nearly dislocating the bard's spine on more than one occasion. "You," he slurred affectionately, pointing with a sausage-like finger, "you're alright, stubby. You sing badly, but you share spirits like a prince of the old kingdoms!"

Galdon smiled through gritted teeth, his spine whispering for mercy. "Why, thank you, mighty Kaldir. Your... enthusiasm is an honor I'll treasure. Truly."

Sniffles leaned toward Micah, whispering from his belly-down position. "He's gonna die, right? I give it one more slap and he folds like a poorly made tent."

Micah was too busy panicking internally to answer. He was already calculating how many coins they didn't have, how many rations they would now have to stretch across four mouths, and worst of all, how much more dwarven singing he'd be forced to endure. His eyes twitched.

"You hear that, lads?" Kaldir bellowed, raising his tankard like a war banner. "We're on a quest! Treasure! Glory! Ale beyond mortal comprehension!"

"And possibly death," Sniffles added helpfully.

"Exactly!" Kaldir cheered. "The quad-squad! Nay—the... the... Fellowship of the Spirits!" He grinned, clearly impressed with himself.

"I'm not wearing matching cloaks," Micah said flatly.

Galdon, now halfway into a slow sideways slide away from Kaldir's elbow zone, chuckled. "Of course not. That's for when we establish our traveling minstrel troupe. Think of the brand potential!"

Sniffles, ever the opportunist, piped up. "If we're splitting treasure four ways now, do we at least get to vote him out if he snores like a stampede again?"

Kaldir didn't hear him. He was busy drawing a battle diagram in the dirt with a stick. It mostly resembled a fork fighting a turnip, but it was clear he was very proud of it.

"I've seen tavern fights that went worse," Galdon muttered.

Micah groaned, burying his face in his hands. "I wanted magic. A tower. Maybe a pet dragon. Not... this."

Just then, a moth flew directly into Kaldir's nostril.

The Minotaur let out a snort so thunderous it nearly extinguished the fire. He stumbled backward into a tree with a grunt, took one last heroic swig from the skin, and passed out face-first into his dirt diagram, turning "victory plan" into a Minotaur-shaped smudge.

Silence followed—a moment of sacred stillness.

Sniffles raised his head and said solemnly, "I vote we steal back the spirits while he's down."

Micah didn't even look up. "Seconded."

And in the firelight, beneath a sky of silent stars, a wizard, a gnome, and a bard quietly tiptoed toward the unconscious embodiment of chaos, now snoring in a tone that could summon earthquakes.

Chapter Thirty Two: Of Headaches and Heists

The four unlikely adventurers assembled once more under the gentle glow of dawn, the early sun painting gold across the forest path like some divine apology for whatever had happened the night before.

Micah and Sniffles nibbled on dry biscuits, their expressions somewhere between sleep-deprived and spirit-crushed. Galdon, the dwarf, maintained a carefully neutral face—one that said, "I am not hungover, I am simply mysterious." Only Kaldir, hulking and groaning like a storm cloud with hooves, was clearly paying the price for last night's liquid bravado.

He stumbled forward, a shade of green not typically found outside of swamps and regret. "No more dwarf spirits," he mumbled to himself. "I swear on my horns. Just water. Sweet, life-giving—does anyone have water?!"

He swung his heavy gaze toward his companions. Micah subtly tucked his waterskin out of sight. Sniffles made himself very interested in a patch of moss.

But then his eyes landed on Galdon.

Still here. Suspicion crept into his sunburnt mind.

What's he still doing here? Maybe... maybe he brought more spirits? Kaldir's face flickered with dangerous hope.

Sensing the scrutiny like a sixth sense (or possibly a survival instinct), Galdon sprang into action.

"Ah, my friend!" he exclaimed, striding over with the confidence of a man who had definitely not just joined this crew on a fabricated invitation. "Thank you for trusting me to be part of your noble quest! I vow to be a true asset to the team." He extended a hand that quivered only slightly under the weight of performance.

Kaldir blinked at him. Then, memory—blurred, bubbly, and fermented—floated to the surface.

"Right... right, I did say that, didn't I?"

With the grace of a crumbling building, Kaldir extended his colossal hand and enveloped Galdon's in a handshake that nearly compressed the dwarf into a decorative coin.

"Welcome aboard," Kaldir said.

Behind them, Micah and Sniffles exchanged identical looks of horror and betrayal. Their expressions could have soured milk from thirty paces.

The group trudged onward into the woods, the trees thickening and shadows stretching like yawns around them. Micah and Sniffles crept a few paces ahead, whispering furiously in a language that might have just been increasingly agitated sighs.

Kaldir, meanwhile, drew closer to Galdon, his voice dropping to a conspiratorial grumble.

"Well, friend... I don't suppose you've got any more of that excellent dwarf brew tucked away?" He patted his aching head for emphasis. "This infernal skullquake's making me consider chewing bark."

Galdon hesitated, the mental gears turning at full throttle.

He had no spirits left. But he had something better: confidence.

Leaning in, he smiled. "Well, I might just know a fella. But it'll cost us a detour, maybe a favor or two."

Kaldir's eyes lit up like tavern lanterns at dusk.

Behind them, Sniffles whispered to Micah, "If that dwarf gets him drunk again, I'm hiding all the firewood."

Micah sighed. "Let's just hope the next detour doesn't include another bush of angry thorns."

"Or pants," Sniffles muttered, adjusting his waistband with a wince.

Chapter Thirty Three: The Slightest Detour

Brooding silence hung over the group like a fog of collective suspicion—thick, cloying, and flavored faintly with the regret of past decisions. Kaldir plodded along the dirt path, every hoofbeat a dull thunk against the earth. His eyes remained fixed on the horizon, but his mind drifted elsewhere, specifically, to barrels of dwarf spirits and the soft giggles of Minotaur maidens who didn't judge a warrior by his belt size.

Behind him, Sniffles and Micah walked with purposeful bounces in their steps, their heads bent together as they studied the ancient map, which may or may not have once doubled as a placemat.

"Looks like the path splits up ahead," Micah said, pointing with his staff. "See here? Jorg's Hold is north through the pass."

Sniffles squinted. "Are you sure? That could just as easily say 'Goats Fold.'"

"I'm ninety percent sure. Maybe eighty-five. Definitely more than fifty."

Before they could resolve the debate—or discover if they were headed toward treasure or livestock—Kaldir, ever the picture of innocent manipulation, clomped to a stop beside the weathered crossroads sign. It pointed north to "Jorg's Hold" and left toward "Blackroot Village."

"Eh, what's the harm in a quick stop?" Kaldir said with exaggerated casualness, beginning to shuffle through their packs. "Let's see what we've got. Rations… dry cheese… something that might once have been fruit but is now a weapon…"

"We're fine on provisions," Micah replied, not looking up. "I think we're good for a while—as long as the dwarf doesn't eat like you—uh, I mean… as long as no one overeats."

Galdon raised an eyebrow. "I'm standing right here, you know."

"But what if we're delayed?" Kaldir pressed, his eyes wide with the innocent gleam of someone plotting an entirely selfish detour. "We've got a new member now. More mouths, more miles. Best to top things up now. And, you know…" He cleared his throat dramatically. "Fill our skins with brew—water. Obviously water."

Sniffles eyed him narrowly. "You said 'brew' first."

"It was a slip of the tongue," Kaldir grunted, hoofing at the dirt like a guilty ox.

Micah glanced between the map and Kaldir, then sighed with the weight of every bad decision he had ever made (and they were many). "It is just a slight detour."

"A left turn!" Kaldir added cheerfully. "Hardly even counts as a detour."

With the reluctant agreement of the party, they packed up their existing, perfectly adequate provisions and followed the winding left path toward Blackroot Village.

Micah and Sniffles trudged side by side, casting wary glances at the minotaur's swaggering tail and whispering mutinous things like, "We're being hoodwinked," and "Next time I get to navigate."

Meanwhile, Galdon strolled behind them all, whistling a dwarven tune and smirking knowingly to himself.

For a quest that promised danger, magic, and destiny… they sure took a lot of snack breaks.

The village was much farther than expected, and they were all squabbling about the long detour. The minotaur tried vainly to defend his decision to go for supplies when they finally reached the village. The sun had already begun to set when they eventually located the village inn. The wizard, angry with the delay of the quest and tired after the long, unnecessary trek, could see Kaldir's eyes brighten in anticipation as he looked at the inn. The wizard was getting used to that look and knew there would be an even longer delay if the Minotaur settled into the common room, and he was having none of it. "The least you can do is buy us a bed for the night!" He stated with fury, "I refuse to go any farther this evening, and I especially refuse to watch you drink yourself into another stupor."

Quite surprised at the little wizard's vehemence, Kaldir readily agreed as he headed straight to the Best Inn and Bar for Miles (at least that is what the sign said). *We'll see*, he thought to himself. "You guys get supplies while I, umm, check out the rooms," he said, tossing them a few coins.

"No way!" the Wizard objected. "We are staying with you. We don't want you blabbing to anyone else about our business!"

"Erm…" Kaldir shifted his eyes with embarrassment, "Well, then, it's settled!" He hastily opened the door of the inn with a loud bang. With a hurried glance around the room, he yelled, "Barkeep! A pitcher of your finest ale for my companions and me," as he headed straight for a corner table where they could keep an eye on all the patrons. The inn was much like The Watering Hole: a cozy fire blazing for warmth and the tantalizing aroma of cooked meat wafting from the kitchen. The only difference was the considerably larger space, which provided ample room to accommodate the many patrons arriving. Gazing around, Micah's eyes locked on the most beautiful human he had ever seen, sitting at the bar, luxurious flaming red hair flowing down her back. Realizing she was watching them make their way to the table, he missed his step and fell face-first into the lap of a rather large, unfriendly-looking traveler as the gnome walked into him from behind.

Micah's face planted squarely in the lap of what could only be described as a professional grumbler. The large, barrel-chested man—whose expression already suggested a lifelong disdain for small talk, mild weather, and wizard-kind—looked down slowly at the unfortunate tangle of limbs sprawled across his thighs.

Micah blinked up at him, face squashed against a belt buckle that smelled faintly of old onions and worse decisions.

"Hello," he squeaked. "Lovely lap—uh, day, isn't it?"

The bar went quiet. Even the fire in the hearth seemed to hold its crackle.

Behind him, Sniffles froze mid-step, one foot on Micah's trailing robe. "Micah…" he whispered in a tone usually reserved for prayers and funeral rites. "Get. Out. Of. His. Lap."

Micah rolled sideways off the man's knees with all the grace of a sack of laundry tumbling off a cart. He popped up, brushing himself off, trying to look like this was all part of his entrance routine.

The man's glare could've turned wine to vinegar. He stood slowly, like a rising storm, and cracked his knuckles with a sound like splintering tree trunks. The room collectively leaned back, anticipating a brawl.

That's when Kaldir stepped in.

Literally.

Between them.

Towering, fur bristling, horns gleaming under the lantern light, Kaldir looked the man dead in the eye and said, "Is there a problem, friend?"

The man, who had expected to tower over most company, found himself chest-to-chest with a walking battering ram who smelled faintly of forge smoke and spilled ale. He wisely reconsidered the direction of his wrath.

"No problem at all," the traveler muttered, backing away slowly, bumping into a chair, and pretending that the whole thing had been a simple misunderstanding. He retreated to the far side of the room and took his beer with him, like it might shield him from further embarrassment.

Sniffles let out a long, whistling exhale. "Well," he said to Micah, "you sure know how to make an entrance."

Micah straightened his robes, eyes darting toward the bar. "Did she see?"

"Oh, she saw," Sniffles muttered. "And I think she's trying very hard not to laugh."

Indeed, Scarlotta—hair like firelight and eyes sharp as silver—was watching them with an amused smirk curling her lips. She raised her glass in a silent toast and returned to her drink, her expression one of curiosity rather than scorn.

"I think she likes me," Micah whispered.

"She probably thinks you're a court jester in training," Sniffles replied.

Kaldir dropped into the corner booth with a grunt. "Next time, try not to dive into angry strangers. Or do. Either way, let me finish my ale first."

As the mugs arrived and the laughter began to filter back into the inn's air, none of them noticed Scarlotta whispering something into her glass, or the subtle shimmer that danced across its surface in response.

The Minotaur had also noticed the pretty woman at the bar, but had no trouble letting her know. He caught her eye and leered, giving her his best smile. She managed not to spew her drink onto the patron beside her and turned her head, shuddering with disgust.

Micah's face had reached a shade of red that closely resembled a boiled beet, though less dignified. Every time his eyes accidentally met the fiery-haired woman's across the bar, he would immediately look away, pretend to examine the grain of the wood on the table, or feign a cough so dramatic it would concern a physician.

Sniffles leaned in conspiratorially, slurping the foam from his mug with exaggerated precision. "If you keep staring at her like that," he said, "someone's going to assume you're trying to curse her with awkwardness."

Micah hissed back, "I am not staring. I am… observing. From a distance. Respectfully. Like a wizard should."

"You're sweating like a frog at a falcon fair," Sniffles said flatly.

"Am I?" Micah patted his forehead with his sleeve and groaned. "Oh, no. I'm glistening like a roasted turnip. This is a disaster."

Across the room, Scarlotta swirled the liquid in her glass with absent grace, lips quirking upward. She was keenly aware of the attention she was receiving. Every calculated glance, every accidental blush—it was all quite… amusing. They always looked at her like that, these men who mistook danger for beauty. She toyed with a silver pendant at her throat and sighed. She hadn't come to this forsaken village to be flirted with by moon-eyed magicians or leered at by minotaurs.

And yet…

There was something about them. Or more accurately, something near them.

Her eyes narrowed, catching the faintest shimmer pulsing from beneath the minotaur's pack. It was subtle—barely more than a flicker—but it was magic. Old, deep magic. And that meant opportunity.

Back at the table, Kaldir had noticed none of this. He was halfway through a roasted shank and most of a pitcher, content in his greasy glory. Galdon, however, had seen the flicker too. His eyes darted to Scarlotta, then to the wizard, then back again.

"Well, well," the dwarf murmured under his breath, stroking his chin. "This night just got a whole lot more interesting."

"Well, this isn't so bad. I think I understand Kaldir now. Just a little more, and maybe I will go see that pretty little thing at the bar." He gulped down the rest of the cup, waved at the server, and yelled in a voice that was beginning to slur. "Another round over here, my good woman!"

The server, decidedly NOT a woman, brought another round to the table and angrily slammed the drinks down. The Minotaur, obviously not getting any attention from the girl at the bar, peered drunkenly at the server and winked his bloodshot eye, leering suggestively. The server, his lip curled in disgust, raised his now-empty tray over his head and aimed it squarely at the Minotaur's furry snout. Belatedly seeing the situation unfold, Galdon quickly rose to his feet and grabbed the server's arm. With the meager coins in his pouch jingling in his other hand, he spoke quietly to the server while leading him away from his companions, thinking maybe this wasn't a good idea after all.

Micah, driven by a sudden jolt of madness—or bravery born of secondhand dwarf spirits—pushed back his chair.

"Oh no," Sniffles said immediately. "Micah, no."

"I must," Micah replied, standing, wobbly but determined.

"No, you really must not," the gnome insisted.

"She looked at me, Sniffles."

"She also looked at the roasted pigeon. Doesn't mean she wants to marry it."

Micah ignored him, straightened his hat, took a deep breath, and began the long, awkward walk toward the bar.

Kaldir finally looked up, chewing with loud disinterest. "Is the wizard about to die? Should I finish his soup?"

Sniffles sighed and held out his hand. "Give it a minute."

With his attention firmly on the pretty girl on the barstool, he did not notice the large traveler from earlier abruptly move his chair closer to his table, thereby protecting his previously disturbed nether region, as he stumbled by. After passing the last table without mishap, Micah did his best drunken saunter up to the bar stool next to the young woman. Using his elbow to steady himself on the bar, he attempted to hop up onto the stool but misjudged the distance and hit the floor soundly with his behind. Jumping up as confidently as possible (as if he meant to do that… while resembling a broken jack-in-the-box), he climbed successfully onto the stool with a hiccup and smiled crookedly at the lady. "Well, hello," he said with another hiccup, "fancy meeting someone as hic, fine as yourself in such an out-of-the-way place."

She looked at the wizard forlornly and responded with a long sigh and a sad smile. "Hello, stranger,"

"Why, hic, do you seem so sad?" Micah asked. "Perhaps my friends and I can be of assis..assis..of help?" He hiccupped.

Good God, he's plastered, it might be to my advantage though, she thought, "I don't know if anyone can." She skillfully brought tears to her eyes. "I have been here for days, desperately looking for a strong, brave man who can help me find my dear cousin."

Scarlotta's eyes glistened convincingly as she brushed a hand through her cascading red curls, playing the part of a distressed damsel with masterful finesse. "My cousin was last seen heading toward the ruins near Jorg's Hold," she murmured, her voice trembling just enough to tug at Micah's intoxicated sympathies. "He went looking for an artifact buried beneath the old crypts. Foolish, really, but he thought it could change our fate…"

Micah's eyes widened, a mixture of wonder and tipsy determination swirling in his gaze. "Well, by my boots and beard trimmings, that's where we're going!" he declared, slapping the bar for emphasis, nearly toppling backward. "We shall find your cousin, madam—er, miss—erm, my lady of mystery!"

Back at the table, Sniffles leaned toward Galdon and whispered, "He's done for."

"Hook, line, and spell-challenged sinker," Galdon agreed, sipping from his mug with a theatrical sigh.

Kaldir, having just noticed the exchange, grunted. "Is she talking about the ruins near the southern peak?"

Galdon nodded. "That's what she told the wizard."

Kaldir's eyes narrowed, not entirely with suspicion, partly with gas—but something about her was setting off the warning bells buried beneath layers of ale and bravado.

Meanwhile, Scarlotta gently laid a hand on Micah's arm, her voice barely above a whisper. "If you truly are a wizard—and your companions are as brave as you claim—then perhaps fate brought us together for a reason…"

Micah, puffing up like a toad with a self-esteem issue, grinned. "Fate indeed! We are the Heroes of the Hold! Well, not officially... yet. But soon!"

And with that, Scarlotta's plan had begun to unfold—one drunken step at a time.

Scarlotta suppressed a grin behind a perfectly executed pout, her fiery red hair cascading forward just enough to veil the glint of triumph in her eyes. So easy. Still, she couldn't help but feel a strange tug—not the usual manipulation-born satisfaction, but a deeper flicker of something else. *What is it about these fools…?* she wondered.

Micah, meanwhile, had turned with a flourish that nearly knocked over the stool. His cape (which was just a repurposed curtain from the tavern they stayed at last week) caught on a splintered edge of the bar, yanking him back like a marionette on a drunken string.

"Right this way, my...fine lady," he slurred, stumbling forward like a hero out of a poorly funded puppet show.

At the table, Sniffles was busy drawing an exceptionally crude map in spilled ale with a sausage link, and Galdon was regaling Kaldir with what appeared to be a completely fabricated tale of single-handedly outwitting a harpy queen, though even Kaldir, half asleep, managed a grunt of skepticism.

When Micah arrived back with Scarlotta in tow, he dramatically threw out an arm (grazing a nearby patron's plate of potatoes) and announced, "Fellow champions of virtue, I present to you Lady…" he blinked, then leaned back and whispered loudly, "Wait, what's your name again?"

Scarlotta gave a subtle, elegant curtsey and said with the elegance of a noblewoman, "Scarlotta. A humble traveler... in need."

The group blinked at her, stunned by her presence-or perhaps because none of them were used to bathing in perfume instead of pond water.

"She's lost her cousin," Micah added. "A caravan. Bandits. A great injustice. We must help."

Kaldir blinked. "She's coming with us?"

Galdon's eyes narrowed. "She smells too nice. What does she really want?"

Sniffles nodded in silent agreement but was too busy trying to wipe the sausage map off his nose to say anything.

And Scarlotta? She smiled sweetly, knowing full well this misfit band might just be her way back to everything she lost.

Or her undoing.

Scarlotta folded her hands demurely and batted her lashes with an air of practiced innocence. "Oh, it's nothing so grand—just a small matter of family. My cousin was last seen traveling with a caravan that vanished near the edge of the Whispering Woods. No one has heard from them since. I fear bandits or worse." She let her voice tremble ever so slightly, though her eyes remained fixed and calculating, scanning each reaction.

Sniffles straightened up, nose twitching suspiciously. "Whispering Woods? That's halfway to the Wyrmlands! I've heard of trees that eat people in those woods!"

Kaldir's ears perked up at the word caravan, which to him meant cargo, which meant possibilities. "Were they transporting anything... valuable?"

Scarlotta paused with the faintest smirk, then let her expression falter, as though stricken with fresh grief. "Just supplies for the village they were headed to. And my cousin's heirloom... a necklace with an opal the color of midnight storms. Family treasure, you understand." She placed a hand over her heart with dramatic flair, as if moved by the memory.

Kaldir gave an approving grunt. "Hmph. Bandits with taste, then."

Galdon narrowed his eyes, unimpressed by her theatrics. "Heirlooms. Vanishing caravans. Half a map and a party of fools. Sounds like the beginning of a bad story."

Scarlotta's eyes snapped to him, and for the briefest moment, her facade slipped. A flash of iron flickered behind her irises. "Some stories are worth the risk, dwarf," she said smoothly. "Especially when one's destiny may lie at the end of them."

Kaldir was nodding, clearly more swayed by her hair than her logic.

Sniffles was still trying to calculate how many things could eat them between here and the Whispering Woods.

And Micah? He let out a loud snore and muttered something about flying goats.

"Well," Galdon muttered, "it's settled then. We're doomed."

Scarlotta smiled and joined the group, her eyes lingering briefly on the little trinket dangling from Kaldir's belt. Her fingers itched, her mind raced, and somewhere deep inside, a forgotten magic stirred.

Did I hear Half a Map?

Yes—you did hear half a map. And the moment Scarlotta caught wind of it, something deep and ancient flickered behind her eyes.

Her fingers tightened imperceptibly around the mug of ale, her mind whirring. *Could it really be…?*

Slipping her hand casually into her cloak pocket, she withdrew a small, timeworn piece of parchment. The edges were uneven, singed in places, and brittle from age. She had carried it for years now, never fully understanding its purpose. It had been given to her by a secretive old witch before the conclave stripped her of her powers—an act done out of fear, not justice. They had called her too strong, too wild, too unpredictable.

They had called her dangerous.

But now, fate had dropped her into a tavern with a drunk minotaur who might be holding the missing half of her map. A wizard who miscasts more than he hits. A gnome thief with a nose you could hang lanterns from. And a bard who likely couldn't carry a tune in a bucket.

In other words… *perfect.*

She glanced at her fragment again. The ink had faded, but the symbols—*oh*, the symbols matched the ones she'd glimpsed carved into the minotaur's strange trinket. Her eyes darted to Kaldir's belt, where it swung like an afterthought.

Could this ragtag crew, this utterly ludicrous collection of misfits, be her key to restoring what was lost?

Of course, they could. Destiny rarely wears a polished boot.

Scarlotta smiled. A slow, knowing, dangerous smile. She folded the paper and tucked it away again with care.

"Well then," she purred, looking over the group, "it seems we're all a little more connected than we thought." Her eyes flicked to the trinket, then to the wizard snoring under the table. "How... fortunate."

Galdon didn't miss the glance. His eyes narrowed. He made a mental note: *Watch the witch.*

Angry—yes—but also curious, Galdon considered the strange offer from Scarlotta. A side trip, he thought. What harm could it do? The Grand Master needn't know… yet. With a grunt of resolve, he turned to ask Sniffles for his thoughts—only to find the gnome was no longer sitting beside him.

"What the—?"

His eyes scanned the room, only to discover the little thief tangled beneath the table with the equally unconscious wizard. Arms and legs were entwined in a desperate tangle for warmth, like a pair of mismatched socks left in the dryer too long. Sniffles' nose was smooshed against Micah's hair, while Micah clutched a table leg as if it were a precious staff.

"Oh, how the tables have turned," Galdon muttered, suppressing a groan.

Just then, a thunderous crash shook the inn.

The dwarf whirled around, just in time to witness the Minotaur, Kaldir, attempting to stand. Unfortunately, his drunken coordination betrayed him. His chair gave way with a violent crack, and he fell backwards like a felled tree, landing beside the gnome and wizard with enough force to rattle mugs off tables.

There was a stunned silence… and then, with drunken determination, Kaldir made himself comfortable, sprawling across the two smaller companions like a giant, furred blanket. A great snore rumbled from his chest a moment later, vibrating the floorboards.

Galdon pinched the bridge of his nose. "What have I gotten myself into?" he groaned aloud.

Gathering what remained of his dignity (and patience), he marched back to the bar where Scarlotta now stood, the very picture of calm— and danger wrapped in silk.

"We'll meet you at the city gates in the morning," he said tersely. "Don't be late."

As he turned to go, he thought he heard a soft, musical chuckle behind him.

Great, he thought bitterly. *She's either amused or plotting how best to devour us in our sleep.*

Either way, he'd have to watch all their backs. But Scarlotta… her brain was already moving faster than any of them could imagine.

And she was several moves ahead.

If I just need the map, Scarlotta mused silently from her perch in the corner of the inn, *then I can continue on my own.*

Her fingers toyed absently with the half-sheet of parchment in her pocket, its faded symbols nearly burned into her memory. *I would certainly prefer it,* she added with a mental sigh. *Heaven knows I work far better without a band of bickering buffoons and drunken beasts.* She cast a sideways glance toward the pile of adventurers snoring under the shattered remains of their table.

The dwarf was already suspicious—too suspicious. His sharp eyes missed little, and his scowl could curdle milk. If she stayed with them, she'd have to play a part constantly. Best to retrieve the other half of the map and vanish. But she wasn't foolish. She'd need muscle—just enough to get her through the next stage. *Mercenaries aren't hard to find in a border town like this.*

Her mind already plotting, she melted into the early morning shadows, slipping out to make a few well-placed inquiries.

Morning came far too quickly for the trio entangled beneath the table. Their first awareness was not of sunlight but of pain—the kind of pain that echoed through the skull and made one question the existence of joy.

"Get up, you lushes. Time to go," Galdon barked, arms crossed, smirking at their misery. The dwarf's tone was filled with far more satisfaction than sympathy.

Micah, Kaldir, and Sniffles groaned as one—three hungover souls fused by poor choices and dwarf spirits. Their eyelids peeled back slowly, lashes crusted with tavern dirt, and their tongues felt like woolen socks stuck to the roofs of their mouths.

Micah attempted a crawl from under the table but only made it halfway before emptying what remained of his stomach in a violent, echoing display of regret. That unfortunate symphony triggered an immediate response from Kaldir and Sniffles, both rolling onto their sides and contributing to the chorus of wretchedness.

The dwarf, proud bearer of a "stomach of steel," paled visibly. As a fresh wave of stench rose like a cloud of doom, even he was forced to beat a hasty retreat to the front stoop, breathing heavily and whispering, "Don't you dare… don't you dare…"

He braced against the doorframe, staring into the bright dawn, regretting every decision that led him to this particular chapter of his life.

Back inside, Micah flopped onto his back, arm over his eyes. "I feel like I got run over by a troll's mother."

"Shhhh," Sniffles moaned. "Not so loud... I can hear my brain trying to escape."

Kaldir grunted from the floorboards, still half-curled around a table leg. "Someone… bring me water. And a new liver."

Outside, Scarlotta stood with her new hires—three ogres. Not so bright, but lots of muscle. She sent them ahead to be ready for the ambush. The game was shifting.

And none of them, least of all the hungover heroes inside, had any clue how quickly it was about to begin.

Rising with the grace of overturned furniture, the wizard leaned on his staff like a newborn foal finding its legs. The gnome clung to the Minotaur's shaggy side, using his fur as a handrail while the trio staggered toward the exit like condemned men shuffling to the gallows.

The second they stepped into the blazing morning light, a unified shriek echoed through the town square:

"AHHHH!"

"My eyeballs are burning!" the wizard wailed in such a pitiful tone that even the usually unflappable dwarf winced in sympathy. Galdon muttered something about "amateur drinkers" and "natural selection" under his breath.

As their vision slowly returned, they found Kaldir with his entire head submerged in a horse trough, scrubbing with a vigor usually reserved for barn floors. With a splash and a triumphant snort, he pulled his dripping head free and declared, "Ah! Much better!"

Inspired by his success, Micah and Sniffles launched themselves into the trough like synchronized swimmers auditioning for a very rural circus. They surfaced moments later, gasping and grinning like fools.

"Brilliant!" Micah beamed. "Note to self—never drink dwarf spirits again!"

The cheerful moment dissolved into dread as flashes from the night before returned—bits of laughter, slurred boasts, a suspiciously vivid memory of a woman with flaming red hair and... considerable assets.

His stomach turned. "Oh no... what did I do?" He scanned the faces around him. "Do we, um, have to do anything today? Other than... you know... heading to Jorg's Hold?"

The dwarf, now thoroughly unimpressed, crossed his arms and growled. "Yes, thanks to your enchanting display of inebriated chivalry, we're now saddled with a helpless damsel—who I suspect wouldn't know helplessness if it sat on her lap and asked for tea."

"She's looking for her cousin," Galdon continued with all the enthusiasm of a tax auditor, "who may or may not exist. And you, you flailing pint-sized romantic, volunteered us. Loudly."

The Minotaur and gnome, once again united in chaos, collapsed into fits of giggles.

Micah's ears turned pink. He glanced around in shame, then perked up. "Scarlotta! I hope she's as pretty as I remember!"

And with the cheerful delusion of a man whose memory was stitched together with ale and optimism, he began skipping toward the town gate, his staff tapping along beside him like a drunken metronome.

The others stood silently for a beat.

"Keep an eye on him," Galdon muttered, stepping forward. "There's something off about that woman. Pretty, yes—but there's power behind those eyes. She's not what she pretends to be."

Kaldir gave a solemn nod.

Sniffles, now entirely composed and ready to defend the wizard's honor—even if he couldn't quite remember what happened—pulled up his trousers and tightened his belt.

"Don't worry," he said, puffing up his chest. "No one's getting past this nose."

They fell into step, trailing their overly eager wizard, who was humming a tune suspiciously close to a romantic ballad.

Scarlotta stood poised at the town gate, the morning sun casting golden light on her crimson hair, now tied back in a loose braid. Her cloak fluttered lightly in the breeze, her face the picture of composed elegance—until she saw them.

She tried. She truly did. But no amount of composure could withstand the sight now approaching her.

Micah was skipping. Not walking, not trotting—skipping—with his robes flapping wildly, his staff nearly tripping him every third bounce as he hummed some absurd, off-key ballad about rescuing fair maidens and enchanted squirrels.

Behind him, the gnome trotted dutifully along, chin high, eyes darting from side to side with exaggerated suspicion, like he expected assassins behind every cabbage cart. He had shoved a slightly wilted daisy into his tunic collar—no one was sure why—and was holding it like a symbol of noble intent.

Then there was the Minotaur.

Kaldir, lumbering forward with a groan in every step, squinted against the sunlight as if it were a personal insult. He still smelled faintly of last night's dwarf spirits, and his left horn had a suspicious smudge of soup on it.

And trailing behind, looking like he regretted every life choice that had brought him here, was the dwarf.

Galdon.

His expression was so grim he might've been marching to his funeral. Again.

Scarlotta bit her lip, desperately trying to maintain her usual mystique, but it was no use. A giggle—light and melodic, wholly unbecoming of her usual calm demeanor—escaped before she could stop it. She clapped a hand over her mouth, eyes wide at herself.

Get a hold of yourself, she scolded silently. *You are Scarlotta Allure—witch, ranger, exiled enchantress. You do not giggle.*

But still… they were so ridiculous.

Her gaze lingered on them, and to her great dismay, the giggle returned—softer this time, but no less real.

What am I doing with these fools? She thought. *And why... why does it feel like I'm exactly where I'm supposed to be?*

She straightened her shoulders, schooling her expression back into cool indifference just as Micah skidded to a stop in front of her, panting lightly and smiling with the pride of someone who had just conquered a minor hill without falling over.

"Good morning, Scarlicious—I mean Scarlotta! Definitely Scarlotta. That's your name. And I am Micah. Again."

Behind him, Sniffles gave a half-bow that looked more like a sneeze, and Kaldir let out a grunt that might have been a greeting—or indigestion.

Galdon just sighed and muttered, "Let's get this over with."

Scarlotta smiled, just a hint of mischief in her eyes.

"Yes," she said smoothly. "Let's."

She was sunlight in silk, lounging against the gatepost as if posing for a bard's ballad. Micah's heart performed an interpretive dance in his chest.

"I am anxious to find the treasure, uh, my cousin." She recovered quickly, but her eyes darted toward the trees for half a heartbeat. Micah didn't notice. He was too busy writing imaginary wedding vows in his head.

Sniffles gave a polite nod but kept one hand on his coin pouch. Kaldir just grunted, his ears twitching slightly in what might've been suspicion—or indigestion.

Galdon didn't say a word, but his eyes narrowed like a trap about to snap. *This one's hiding more than a cousin,* he thought.

Oblivious to everything but the glowing goddess beside him, Micah chattered nonstop, his words tumbling over each other like eager puppies. He clasped Scarlotta's hand in a grand flourish and practically skipped ahead, dragging her in the wake of his romantic delusion. He tried whispering an enchantment he'd made up on the spot—'Affectionis Eternia!'—but all it did was tangle his shoelaces.

With practiced grace, Scarlotta slipped free of his grip as he floundered with his shoelaces. She glanced at him with a tight-lipped smile, fingers flexing as if resisting the urge to push him into a bush. She lengthened her stride to walk beside the dwarf instead. Galdon didn't look at her. He didn't need to. His stiff shoulders and glaring silence said enough.

Unfazed, she turned her charm on the minotaur. "It's just up the road," she offered smoothly, her voice a soft melody. "East, into the Infernal Forest. There's a small path to the right—it'll take us there."

Kaldir grunted and drifted over to the dwarf, muttering something in a low voice. Galdon's eyes narrowed, scanning the trees as if they were listening.

As the party neared the worn, narrow trail, a hush seemed to settle over them—birdsong faded, wind still. The dwarf raised a hand. "Stay sharp," he growled.

Each companion gave a nod. Even Kaldir's ears twitched slightly.

Except for Micah, who had now taken to staring longingly at Scarlotta's hair as though it held the secrets of the universe.

He trailed behind her, murmuring poetic nonsense about "flame-kissed destiny" and "the amber horizon of your gaze."

Galdon led all business. Sniffles followed, nose twitching. Kaldir lumbered close behind, a hand near his axe.

Scarlotta drifted at the back, her hushed conversation with Micah light and airy—utterly meaningless.

The path narrowed. The forest grew darker, with a dead silence, twisted trees, and unnatural stillness—all foreshadowing the ambush ahead.

"Something's off," Galdon muttered.

"You don't say," Kaldir grunted. "Pretty girl shows up, you lot forget how to use your eyes."

The wizard, still floating in a cloud of imagined romance, mentally composing love ballads involving moonlight, magic, and matching robes, noticed nothing but the vision beside him.

The clearing felt wrong—too quiet, too staged. No birds. No wind. Just the faint creak of leather and Micah's ridiculous laugh trailing behind them.

Galdon turned, brows furrowing. "Scarlotta—?"

He froze.

The witch stood with her dagger pressed to Micah's throat, eyes gleaming with something colder than steel.

"That's my dagger!" Sniffles squeaked indignantly—then blinked. "Wait—WHAT?!"

From the shadows, trees parted like theater curtains—and in lumbered a troupe of ogres. Their stink hit like a rotten onion wrapped in swamp socks, and their grins dripped with cruel delight. They thumped clubs into their palms with the practiced boredom of bullies used to easy work.

Micah whimpered like he was the only person ever betrayed by his one true love.

Galdon stepped forward, voice like crushed gravel. "You're gonna regret touching one hair on his foolish little head.

"This isn't up for discussion," Scarlotta growled, "Hand over the map, or I'll make a necklace from your wizard's teeth."

True to his name, Sniffles began to sniffle. At first, it was just a tremble in his nose. Then a hiccup. Then—like a dam breaking—it erupted into full-on, chest-heaving sobs. The ogres stared at him, blinking in confusion. Then one of them lumbered up to give him a used handkerchief, causing Sniffles to freeze in fright.

Kaldir, visibly mortified, jabbed an elbow into the gnome's ribs. "Get a hold of yourself," he muttered.

Galdon groaned and muttered under his breath, "So much for standing our ground."

Sniffles blew his nose—an act that produced a trumpet blast and a small puff of dust from his sleeve. The ogres recoiled slightly. One scratched its head with a club.

"I need that map," Galdon growled, teeth clenched. *That damned wizard will boil me in owl spit if I come back without it,* he thought grimly.

He squared his shoulders. "And what if we refuse?" he challenged, trying his best to sound like a dwarf who hadn't just been outnumbered five-to-one and outclassed by an armchair villainess with lovely hair.

Scarlotta's eyes sparkled with amusement. "Let's just say," she purred, her dagger pressing deeper into Micah's neck, "your legend as the 'four great adventurers' will be reduced to a cautionary tale of poor decision-making and tragic hygiene."

The ogres grinned—wide, crooked, and entirely too enthusiastic. It was the kind of smile that could scare their grandmothers into cardiac arrest.

Micah squirmed in her grasp. Desperate to escape, he writhed like a greased ferret, only to spin himself halfway around, face-first into a soft, pillowy reality.

"Oh no, no, no!" he yelped internally. Focus! Focus on not dying!

Before he could think too hard about what exactly his nose had just collided with, Scarlotta spun him around with the finesse of a bouncer ejecting a drunk bard. The dagger bit harder into his throat, silencing any further heroics.

Twig the sprite suddenly appeared out of nowhere, launching a completely ineffective but extremely flashy attack.

Micah, trembling in Scarlotta's grip, stealthily fumbled through his robe pockets. His fingers brushed against a few questionable ingredients—*was that a bat's eyelash? A pickle seed? Never mind.* He had a good idea what they were. Probably.

Muttering incantations under his breath with all the stealth of a sneezing goose, he cast what he hoped was a sleep spell.

It was not.

Unbeknownst to him, what he thought was a "string of the evening" was, in fact, a hair of a harpy. Instead of a soothing slumber, a ripple of wild magic sparked outward—and directly into one of the ogres.

The ogre twitched.

Then he giggled.

Then it escalated—deep, guttural, snorting laughter that curdled blood and ruptured eardrums. His belly bounced like a sack of spoiled pudding. The sound, not mention the sight, was so hideous, so unholy, it made the remaining ogres recoil in alarm.

Sniffles clutched his ears. "MAKE IT STOP!"

Kaldir groaned. "He's laughing like a banshee gargling marbles!"

Then, with a thunderous blorp, the ogre unleashed a flatulent eruption worthy of folklore. A noxious green cloud enveloped the clearing, sending birds screaming from the trees.

As if driven by some divine comedy, the ogre, still consumed by laughter, wandered off into the woods—his chuckles echoing between the trees like a nightmare nursery rhyme.

Legend has it that he still laughs to this day. But that's another story.

The remaining ogres stood slack-jawed, still reeling from the cacophony and chemical warfare left in their companion's wake. The minotaur snarled low in his throat, gripping his axe. The dwarf planted his feet, adjusting into a stance so solid it could anchor a ship. Sniffles, meanwhile, was a puddle of despair and snot, rocking and sobbing for his helpless, hiccupping friend.

And yet, all of them kept one hand over their nose. The green haze lingered like a curse.

Seeing his gnome companion in such turmoil, Galdon finally relaxed his stance. His eyes locked on the wizard, then on the dagger pressed to his throat.

"Give us the wizard," Galdon growled, voice laced with reluctant steel. "We'll give you the map in return."

Scarlotta cocked her head. "Hmm. No. I think he'll stay with me until I've seen that map with my own two eyes."

"Absolutely not—" Galdon began, but Sniffles stepped forward, trembling, holding the parchment out with both hands.

"Please," he croaked, his voice thick with guilt. "Please, just give him back."

Sighing with fury and frustration, the dwarf snatched the map and stepped forward cautiously.

"That's far enough," Scarlotta warned, nodding toward one of her ogres. "You—fetch it."

The ogre lumbered toward Galdon, club tapping rhythmically against his hand like a metronome of menace. He took the map and, with deliberate malice, pivoted just enough to bump the dwarf with his massive shoulder, sending Galdon sprawling backward into Sniffles.

The dwarf sprang up with a snarl, fists clenched. "That bloated troll-wart—"

"Easy," Kaldir murmured, placing a massive hand on his shoulder. "We need to get the wizard back."

After a moment's struggle, Galdon nodded tightly.

Scarlotta's eyes gleamed with triumph as she unrolled the brittle parchment, fingers trembling with anticipation. But the moment the map was fully opened, its surface shimmered like moonlight on black water. Strange runes rearranged themselves across the parchment, pulsing with a soft, ominous glow.

The smirk faded from her lips.

"What is this?" she hissed, holding the map up to the fading light. "Why won't it show me anything?"

The ogres stepped back uneasily. Even their dim wits recognized dangerous magic when they saw it.

Galdon leaned toward Kaldir. "It's bound to us," he whispered. "The map's tied to our presence. She can't read it without us."

Scarlotta growled in frustration. She clenched her jaw, face tightening into a mask of cold resolve.

Before anyone could move, she lunged.

Micah yelped as she seized him by the collar of his robe, her dagger once again pressed close to his throat—not drawing blood, but close enough that he froze like a frightened squirrel.

"I'm not finished!" she snarled, dragging him backward.

"Hey!" Sniffles shouted, sprinting forward, but Kaldir's outstretched arm halted him. The Minotaur's eyes were narrowed, calculating.

"Don't follow me," Scarlotta spat. "Not yet. I'll find out what this map is hiding—and I'll see if it matches mine." Her other hand fumbled in her satchel, pulling out a crumpled half-sheet of parchment, which shimmered faintly in response to the map still lying in the grass.

"That wasn't the deal!" roared Galdon, his voice echoing through the clearing like a war drum.

Scarlotta didn't flinch. "I'm a scoundrel and a thief, dwarf. My word means nothing." Her smile was razor-thin and full of menace. "Now… we're leaving. Boys?"

The ogres, already looming behind the trio, moved with synchronized brutality. Before any could react, clubs descended like thunderbolts.

CRACK.

Sniffles crumpled like a discarded cloak, Galdon hit the ground with a grunt of fury, and Kaldir dropped to one knee before collapsing beside them with a moan. The clearing fell eerily silent, but for the crunching of leaves beneath Scarlotta's boots as she turned to Micah.

"Why did you do that?" Micah whispered, horror plastered across his face. "My friends… they trusted you. They did as you asked."

Tears streamed down his cheeks as he knelt by their unmoving forms, his voice breaking. "Why would you hurt them?"

"I can't have three bumbling idiots ruining my plans," she snapped. "I went to great lengths to find this map—sacrificed more than you can imagine. You, little wizard, are the only one I need now."

Scarlotta stepped forward—and then, she hesitated.

Kaldir's massive form lay awkwardly, one horn digging into the dirt. Sniffles' tiny limbs were tangled like discarded twigs, his oversized nose pressed against the ground. Galdon, despite the blow, still clutched his lute close, as if guarding the only part of himself not already broken.

A memory flickered—unbidden, unwelcome. A younger Scarlotta, standing over a fallen comrade, her hands trembling with indecision, her coven retreating behind her. She had made the wrong choice that time, too, and left someone behind. And paid dearly.

Her breath caught.

Just a heartbeat.

She blinked it away.

"Move," she hissed to Micah, her voice harder now, the moment gone—but a seed of doubt buried deep.

Micah's shoulders slumped, doubt washing over him. Maybe she was right. They hadn't accomplished anything without chaos. Perhaps he didn't belong out here, pretending to be something he wasn't. He cast one last worried glance at his friends.

"So," Scarlotta growled, gripping his arm with a strength that belied her frame. "I assume you know where this map leads?"

Micah gave a trembling nod.

"No tricks," she warned, her eyes cold. "No shenanigans. Or your next nap will be permanent."

Scene: Deep in the Forest, Moments After Scarlotta's Betrayal

The map in Scarlotta's hand pulsed weakly, then dulled.

She turned it over. Again. Again. Shook it. Nothing.

She gritted her teeth, furious. "Useless," she snarled. "Useless!"

Micah, crumpled nearby, dared to lift his head. "It only worked when we were all together," he said softly. "It reacts to the group."

That was the wrong thing to say.

In one smooth motion, Scarlotta spun toward him, dagger raised—not striking, but close enough to make him flinch and crawl backward, scraping his palms on root and stone.

"Don't lie to me, boy," she hissed.

His eyes, wide and trembling, glistened. "I'm not!" he whimpered. "I don't know how it works. Please…"

She froze.

That look. Raw, startled fear. The helpless tremble of someone expecting pain, not mercy.

And just like that, the forest faded. She was back in the Conclave's tower, fifteen years old again, fists bloodied from pounding on the steel door of the vault. Her magic was stolen. Her name was condemned. The torches outside flickered as they walked away, leaving her with nothing but silence and fear.

Her grip on the dagger faltered.

Micah watched, confused, as her knuckles loosened and her breathing slowed. The fury was gone, replaced by something else. Something haunted.

Scarlotta stared down at the map in her hand.

"It's not just about the treasure," she whispered, as if confessing to the air itself. Then she turned away sharply, the moment buried as quickly as it had surfaced.

Scene: Awakening in the Aftermath

"Oh, my head," Galdon groaned, wincing as pain ricocheted through his skull like a dwarven war drum. He rolled to his side and slowly pushed himself to his knees, muttering ancient oaths under his breath. Blinking through the blur, he spotted the hulking form of Kaldir sprawled like a toppled statue, and Sniffles curled up like a discarded cloak.

Staggering upright, Galdon limped to their side and gave the minotaur a firm shake. "Hey, you breathing under there?"

Kaldir stirred with a grunt. "Ughhh… I feel worse than I do after three skins of Dwarf Spirits. And that's saying something." He clutched his temple like it owed him gold.

Sniffles whimpered and blinked his teary eyes open. His bottom lip quivered dangerously. "Micah…" he sniffed.

"Oh no, not again," Galdon grumbled. But catching the heartbreak in the gnome's face, he relented, kneeling beside him. "Look, lad. Micah needs you. We've got to find him before that witch wrings what's left of his wits out through his ears."

He gave Sniffles a stiff pat on the shoulder—dwarven affection at its highest form. The gnome sniffled, nodded bravely, and wiped his nose on a sleeve that should've been retired seasons ago.

Kaldir pulled himself upright and squinted toward the rising sun. "We know where they're headed. If we cut through the valley I saw on the map—before Micah lost it—we can get ahead of them. Maybe set up an ambush."

Galdon stroked his beard. "Risky, but it might work. That terrain's rough. We'll need to be quick."

The trio set off, bruised but determined. The valley path was dense with brambles thick enough to make a badger curse. Kaldir drew his great sword with a grunt and began to hack a path, swinging like a farmer with a vengeance.

Sweat beaded on his brow, soaking his fur and glinting in the morning light. Then—a hand. Small, calloused, and unexpectedly gentle, reaching past his side with a leather water skin.

Kaldir turned and stared.

Sniffles stood there, eyes shy but steady, offering him a drink.

Kaldir took it with a grunt of thanks and tipped it back—and nearly dropped it in shock. "By the Forgefather's beard… is this—?"

"The laughing ogre's brew," Sniffles said with a mischievous twinkle. "Snatched it right off him while he was gasping on the ground."

Kaldir let out a bellow of delighted laughter that echoed through the trees. Galdon chuckled too, thumping the gnome on the back.

"Good job, little thief," he said with honest pride.

Sniffles smiled—bright, proud, and for the first time since Micah's capture, full of hope.

Scene: Edge of the Infernal Forest – Entering the Valley of Despair

After hours of slogging through twisted brambles, hidden roots, and more than a few muttered curses, the three weary adventurers finally reached the edge of the Infernal Forest. The late afternoon sunlight cast the towering trees in a golden halo, their canopy lush and welcoming— almost too welcoming.

"Looks… pleasant," Sniffles offered hesitantly, squinting up at the dappled light.

"That's always a bad sign," Galdon muttered.

They pressed on.

The further they descended the valley slope, the more the forest changed. The birdsong vanished. Insects no longer buzzed. Even the breeze seemed to hold its breath. The thick green canopy remained, but beneath it, no underbrush grew. No flowers bloomed. No animal tracks marred the earth.

Instead, the ground was littered with odd, misshapen mounds—haphazard, uneven, and disturbingly unnatural. They rose like silent warnings, untouched by time or weather.

"Ummm," Galdon finally said, his voice hushed. "What did you say this place was called?"

"I didn't," Kaldir replied, his brow furrowed. "I only saw the map once or twice. I think it was the Valley of Desper… Despair… something like that."

Galdon stopped dead in his tracks.

"The Valley of Despair?" he whispered.

Kaldir brightened slightly. "Yes! That sounds right."

"Oh no," Galdon groaned, eyes darting to the mounds. "That's very wrong. This is one of the last places we should ever set foot in."

Sniffles paused mid-step, one boot hovering nervously above a suspicious-looking clump of moss. "Why? What's so bad about… a little despair?"

Galdon turned to him, solemn. "My people know of places like these. We find them sometimes while tunneling near the surface—ancient places. Cursed places. Dead places. We don't talk much about them, and we never stay long."

Kaldir's ears twitched, his nostrils flaring as he sniffed the air. "I smell… nothing. No decay. No animals. Not even rot."

"That's because this place doesn't let things rot," Galdon said grimly. "It traps them."

Scene: The Whispers Beneath the Soil

The air shifted as they passed the threshold into the valley's heart. It was cooler—unnaturally so—and the silence pressed on their ears like wool packed in too tight. Even the ever-chirping Sniffles was unusually quiet, his wide eyes scanning the strange, uneven mounds that dotted the ground like forgotten graves.

"I don't like this," Galdon muttered, fingering the hilt of his small utility axe.

"It's just dirt," Kaldir grunted, kicking a mound dismissively.

The dirt mound hissed.

Everyone froze.

A faint whisper followed, not from above or around, but below.

"Did… did anyone else hear that?" Sniffles asked

The whisper rose again, this time forming fragments of words— barely perceptible, as though the wind itself were remembering how to speak.

"He fell here... they left her behind... still watching... always watching..."

Suddenly, one of the mounds shifted. Slowly. A crack opened in the earth like a gaping mouth, exhaling the scent of old death and rotting sorrow.

From within, a translucent figure clawed its way into the fading light.

It was a woman—or had been, once. Wisps of long, decaying hair floated around a half-skeletal face that blinked slowly, eyeless and weeping tar. Her mouth did not move, but her voice echoed in their minds.

"Why did they leave me?"

Sniffles fell backward with a squawk, landing in a patch of thorny roots. Kaldir instinctively raised his weapon—but found his arms heavy, sluggish, as though invisible hands were dragging him downward.

The spirit floated toward them, pausing before each in turn. But when she came to Galdon, she stopped.

"You remember this place. Your kind watched us fall and tunneled away."

Galdon paled.

"I—I didn't know… I wasn't there—" he started, but she screamed.

It wasn't a normal scream—it was grief, rage, betrayal, and pain woven into a single psychic shockwave. The trees bent inward. The sky dimmed to a sickly green. The forest moaned with her fury.

Just as she raised her arms—spectral claws dripping with shadow— Twig burst from Sniffles' satchel (where he had been hiding) and screamed, "I'M TOO CUTE TO DIE!"

The spirit paused.

Twig blinked.

"So are they!" he added with desperation, gesturing toward the group. "Just… in a tragic, confused way!"

Galdon, without knowing why, desperate in a way he had never felt before, started humming in his gravelly voice. The normal screech that made the others' ears curl was missing. The sound was ancient, powerful, deep, and compelling. The ghost paused in her advance. After a moment, Galdon added words to the song, the sound echoing in the valley.

The ghost tilted her head. The sorrow in her face softened. She drifted backward, her voice fading like a lullaby sung to no one. The mound sealed itself with a final sigh and transformed into what appeared to be a stone slab, which was emitting a very pale light. It was covered with engravings of creatures, most of which none of the party had seen in real life, and what appeared to be writing in some ancient language.

Silence returned.

Kaldir cleared his throat. "So… how about we never talk about this again?"

"Agreed," Galdon muttered.

Twig hopped up on a rock and declared, "You're all welcome! I've saved your bony behinds! Hero status: confirmed."

Sniffles was still curled up in a ball.

The valley seemed quieter now, but not in a way that comforted—it was the kind of silence that swallowed sound, where even breath felt like a trespass.

The companions sat in a rough circle beneath a gnarled, petrified tree, its twisted limbs arched like a protective claw above them. Sniffles poked at the ground with a stick, his nose unusually still. Kaldir paced with twitchy frustration, casting mistrustful glances at every whisper of wind.

The grove had gone still.

Where moments ago the wind had howled, and the trees had groaned with unseen torment, now only silence remained—deep and reverent.

Galdon stood frozen, the last notes of the ancient song hanging in the air like mist. The humming relic, half-buried beneath roots and moss, pulsed softly with pale blue light. It was shaped like a crescent stone tablet, etched with glyphs too old for any tongue spoken in modern taverns.

Twig floated close to it, his glow flickering in rhythmic pulses that matched the beat of the relic's light. His wings, normally erratic and jittery, now fanned gently as if in reverence.

"I didn't know I remembered the words," Galdon muttered, more to himself than anyone. "It was a song my grandmother used to hum… when I was a beardling. Said it was the song of the Weeping Stone. I thought it was just a lullaby…"

Twig turned slowly, his eyes wide and luminous. For the first time, his normally squeaky voice dropped to something quieter, ancient— almost otherworldly.

"Not a lullaby. Key."

He stared out into the darkness where the spirits had risen—their hollow eyes, the way they'd called him by name in tongues older than the stone halls of his ancestors. Words only dwarves of the deepest kin-blood would understand.

He hadn't known what they meant, not entirely. But he had felt it—an aching, ancestral pull in his chest, like a thread woven into the foundations of the world had been tugged. And it frightened him.

"That voice..." he muttered aloud, barely above a whisper.

Twig, who had been oddly quiet throughout the encounter, fluttered forward and hovered near Galdon. The sprite's glow was soft, golden, like lanternlight in a foggy mine. "They knew you," Twig said gently. "Not just who you are. Who you were."

Galdon's brows furrowed. "Aye. That's what scares me."

"You weren't always just a bard, were you?" Twig's voice was kind, not accusing. "There's an echo in your voice when you sing. Like someone else... used to know the song."

Galdon looked away. "There are stories in my clan—old songs, forbidden to those not of pure blood. I used to hear them in my dreams... Now I think they were more than that."

Twig hovered closer, placing a tiny hand on the dwarf's shoulder. "Maybe the songs remember you, too. Maybe that's why they called you." The sprite tilted his head with a mischievous smile. "Could be you're more than a mediocre bard with a thief's conscience and a bruised ego."

Galdon chuckled, hollow but grateful. "Coming from a glowing lightning bug, that almost means something."

Twig smiled brighter, literally, and zoomed up to the branches above. "Well then, you'd better survive long enough to find out."

As the others watched, Twig lit the twisted branches above, casting soft warmth that pushed the chill of despair back just enough to let them sleep.

Twig hovered closer to the relic, placing a tiny hand on its smooth surface. A flare of light surged from within him—gold and soft and warm. The companions stepped back, shielding their eyes.

When it faded, they saw him hovering still… but glowing more brightly than they had ever seen. His form was sharper, his wings steadier.

Sniffles whispered, "Twig… you look… whole."

Twig nodded. "A long time ago, I lived here. Before the Despair came. I stayed too long. Got dim. I forgot who I was until you came."

Kaldir, uncharacteristically solemn, crossed his arms. "What does that make you then? A ghost? A guide?"

Twig smiled with a glow that warmed the edges of their chilled hearts. "A guardian. Of hope. And giggles." He cocked his head, a more serious look on his face. "Mostly hope."

Scene: Visions of the Lost Hold

As night draped the Valley of Despair in a veil of silence, the group clustered around a small fire—its warmth weak against the still-churning memories of the spirits they had encountered.

Twig, fluttering gently above the flames, pulsed with a soft bioluminescent glow—no longer dim, but strong and steady. The sprite landed lightly on a mossy rock, his wings folding back like delicate glass shutters.

"I think you're ready," Twig said, his voice unusually solemn. "You've resisted the valley's sorrow longer than most. I can show you something—but you won't all see the same thing."

The party exchanged glances, curiosity outweighing hesitation.

Twig lifted his tiny hands. From the air around them, a shimmer coalesced—like dew catching first light. It spread, rippling outward, and suddenly, they were no longer in the valley.

Sniffles' vision:

He walks the market square, bustling with cheerful dwarves, gnomes, and humans alike. No one stares at his nose. Instead, children beg him to tell stories, to teach them his tricks. A woman touches his arm fondly, calling him "Master Snout." His eyes well up with tears.

Kaldir's vision:

He enters a glorious mead hall carved into the mountain, filled with roaring laughter, clinking tankards, and kin who slap his back and chant his name. He isn't just welcome—he is honored. His clan leader lifts a horn to him, saying, "You found your way home."

Micah's vision:

Even though separated from the party, Micah also dreams…. He stands in a grand library of glowing crystal shelves—arcane symbols dancing in the air. Magic hums through the floor, pulsing in time with his heartbeat. Somehow, he knew this was Jorg's Hold as a bastion of learning and wonder, not the broken ruin it had become. In the distance, he sees himself—older, surer, surrounded by students.

Galdon's vision:

He stands before a dais in a solemn stone chamber. Etchings on the walls pulse as he sings. The echoes answer with ancient harmony. Dwarves kneel. A voice whispers: "You carry the song of our fathers. It has waited long." His fingers tremble as he realizes the song is not just a melody—it's a key.

Twig's truth:

Unseen by the others, Twig glimpses himself in the ancient hall of Jorg's Hold—light burning like a beacon from his chest. Other sprites fly around him, bright and joyful. He remembers: he was once a guardian of the Hold's emotional heart, dimmed when despair claimed the valley.

As the visions fade, they blink and stare at one another, silent with the weight of what they've seen.

The group stood silently. Even Galdon seemed unsure what to say.

And beneath that odd glow—half-flicker, half-memory—Galdon hummed a tune. Old. Unearthed. Ancient.

The spirits of the valley didn't return that night.

Somewhere, a portal began to open.

From the hill above, just out of sight, Scarlotta watched. She had followed them. She had seen the curse of the Valley try to swallow them. She had seen them stumble, yes—but not break.

And now… this?

Her grip tightened on the branch beside her, jaw clenched. She'd tried to brave this place alone once. It had nearly killed her. She had screamed in the darkness for help. None had come.

But they had each other. And they had… him. That ridiculous glowing sprite.

For the first time in years, Scarlotta felt something unfamiliar flutter in her chest.

Not envy. Not hatred.

Doubt.

She stepped back into the shadows, back to Micah.

From the shadows, far beyond the firelight, Scarlotta watches. Her expression is unreadable. These fools, this broken bunch… yet they withstood the curse together. She had tried alone and failed.

For the first time, she doubts her choice.

Scarlotta's vision

That night, long after Micah had drifted into a restless sleep beside the campfire, and the ogres snored like thunderclouds scattered through the trees, Scarlotta sat alone on a moss-covered rock, map spread across her knees. The stars above blinked down through the canopy like a thousand quiet watchers.

She touched the glowing threads of the map again—still cold, still unyielding. And then…

A pulse.

A heartbeat—not hers. A shimmer ran across the parchment, and in the blink of an eye, the forest faded around her.

Suddenly, she was somewhere else.

Stone walls. Cold. Distant chanting echoes through ancient halls. She was young—barely more than a girl—standing in the center of a vast circular chamber deep within the Conclave's vault. Her arms were bare, trembling. Around her, robed figures chanted, their faces hidden, their judgment absolute.

"Too powerful…"

"Too unpredictable…"

"Too dangerous to let loose."

She remembered the feeling of being unraveled. Of magic being pulled from her bones like threads from a tapestry. Of falling—inside herself—and landing in silence.

And worst of all, the loneliness.

They had locked her away for a time, "for the safety of all," they said. She had cried out for someone to believe her. To believe she wasn't evil. That her power wasn't born of corruption but of pain—and potential.

But no one had come.

Back in the present, Scarlotta gasped and clutched her chest.

The forest returned in a rush, firelight flickering, owls calling softly in the distance. She stared down at the map. The lines still glowed faintly—fainter than before.

Her hands trembled.

She looked over at Micah—curled in the grass, snoring softly with a pinecone stuck in his hair—and she saw something she hadn't allowed herself to feel in years:

Guilt.

Not because he was a threat. But because he wasn't. None of them were.

They were clumsy, annoying, and hopelessly unequipped.

But… they had stood by each other in the Valley of Despair and had risked their lives for one another—something she hadn't done—for anyone—for a long time.

Scene: Micah

Hands tied behind his back, securely attached to a stake in the ground, Micah wondered why he couldn't move his arms. Micah's head swam with confusion. His beautiful Scarlotta had held a dagger to his throat, not just any dagger, his good friend Sniffles' dagger!

I must demand to know how she acquired that from him, unless he gave it to her as a present, why that little sneak, how dare he try to steal my girl? But no, he looked as surprised as I; there must be something else. Let me think this through. We were walking down the path, and we held back together. I thought she wanted to be alone. The others came into the clearing ahead, and she pulled me close. I thought, Oh boy! This is it, um, I have no idea what to do!

Turns out she had it under control, she whirled me around and deftly pulled a dagger from her belt and held it to my throat. I thought to myself, I'm not entirely sure how humans, umm, he blushed just thinking about it, *but I don't think this is how they go about it. The next thing I know, there are the ugliest ogres ever coming out of the forest. Sniffles is well, sniffling, I have my head buried in these soft mounds of, (stop*

*thinking about that!), I cast a spell, and it went pretty well. That ogre
sure was funny,* he thought with a smile on his face. *Oh, yeah,* his face
began to grow darker with remembrance. *She made my friends (and the
dwarf) give her the map, and had the ogres clobber them on the head!*

"Hey, you!" He yelled, searching around for Scarlotta, "Hey, hey,
where are you? Help! Help!" He started screaming loudly, "I've been
abducted by a bunch of big, gross, warty, ugly ogres! Help! Help! Oh,
the smell, please, help me!!!"

"Is this how all grand adventures go?" he mumbled, more to
himself than anyone else. "First the nymph incident, now bondage by
betrayal. If there's a third act, it better come with pie."

His mind began to wander—something it was particularly good at
under pressure. Was this part of some ancient initiation rite for
becoming a great wizard? Or maybe a cosmic punishment for that time
he turned the headmaster's wig into a living squirrel? (It had only lasted
three hours. Well, five.)

Twisting again with a grunt, he found the effort as useful as a
sponge in a sword fight.

Then came a voice—Scarlotta's, sharp and dispassionate. "Stop
writhing. You'll chafe your wrists, and I need you alive."

"Oh, well, thank you for that tender concern," Micah said, sarcastic
even in defeat. "I'll be sure to list it in my memoirs.

She crouched beside him, one eyebrow raised. "You're lucky you're
useful. If that map doesn't reveal its secret soon…" she trailed off, her
fingers brushing the worn parchment she'd taken.

Micah's gaze locked on the map, which still refused to glow, whisper, or do any of the dramatic things maps in stories were supposed to do. Maybe it liked him better. Perhaps it needed... friendship. Or snacks.

Scarlotta stepped fully into view, her hair pulled back now, face half-shaded by the hood she hadn't worn earlier. There was no smirk on her lips, no mocking twinkle in her eye—just that same unreadable mask she wore when no one was looking. The firelight from their dwindling camp cast strange shadows on her face, and for just a flicker of a moment, Micah thought she looked... sad?

"They're alive," she said, voice cool as streamwater but lacking the venom it once carried. "And if they're half as thick-skulled as they act, they'll be up and trudging along by sunrise."

Micah squinted at her, still very much tangled in his bindings, chin tilted defiantly. "That's not good enough. You hit them over the head with clubs! Clubs! Have you ever been clubbed? I bet you haven't. I bet it's terrible!"

He wiggled his arms with as much dignity as one could while trussed up like a roasting goose. "I thought... I thought you liked me. We were holding hands!"

Scarlotta raised one eyebrow. "You grabbed my hand."

"I'm very charming when I panic!"

Her lips twitched—was that almost a smile?

Micah huffed, voice lower now, wounded. "You're just like the rest of them. You pretended to care, and then—" He swallowed hard. "And then you used us."

Scarlotta's expression tightened. Something flickered in her eyes. She looked away, as if studying the trees for answers. "You don't know what it's like," she said finally, voice quieter than he'd ever heard it. "To have something stolen from you. Something inside. To be told you're too dangerous, too powerful, too much. To have your magic ripped away—not because you failed, but because they were afraid of you."

She turned to him again, kneeling now, and for the first time, her eyes weren't guarded—they were haunted.

"It's not just about treasure, Micah," she murmured, barely above a whisper. "This map… it might be the only way to get back what they took from me."

Micah, blinking rapidly, felt the anger in his chest stutter. His mouth opened, then shut again. A beat passed.

"…Okay," he said, awkwardly. "Still doesn't explain the ogres."

Scarlotta actually laughed—a small, dry laugh that faded fast. She stood, brushing off her knees. "Sleep while you can. We move at first light."

Micah thought with a smile on his face—until he remembered the thunderous thwack that followed. The smile dropped. His friends—his real, actual friends—had been knocked out cold because of her.

He wriggled his wrists again. Nothing. The rope had been enchanted, no doubt, because normal rope wouldn't have held him for long. He had spells, after all. Not that they usually did what they were supposed to, but still.

Maybe this is all part of the plan, he reasoned hopefully. *Maybe she just needed to make it look like she betrayed us, and later she'll free me, and we'll laugh about it over stew and starlight, and maybe—*

"Stop it," he muttered to himself. "You're being an idiot. Again."

A shadow moved nearby, breaking through the moonlight. Scarlotta stepped into view, her long cloak whispering around her like mist. She crouched beside him, her silhouette glowing faintly in the moonlight—and for a moment, just a moment, Micah thought he saw something vulnerable in her expression. Tired. Haunted.

"Are you going to untie me?" he asked hopefully.

"No," she said flatly. "You'd just try to cast another spell and turn my kneecaps into cantaloupes or something."

"I got one ogre to run away laughing," he said proudly. "I mean… it wasn't what I meant to do, but still. Pretty impressive."

She smirked. Then it faded. Her gaze drifted to the ground, distant.

"Did you mean to hurt us?" Micah asked quietly. "Or was that just a bonus?"

Scarlotta didn't answer right away. When she spoke, her voice was softer, tinged with something unreadable.

"I've had a lot taken from me. My home. My powers. My name, in a way." She paused, as if choosing the next words carefully. "This map… it might be the only way to get it back. I didn't come looking for you—but somehow, the key led me straight to your little band of misfits."

"We're not misfits," Micah said defensively. Then, sheepishly: "Well, I mean, technically we are, but we're functional misfits. Mostly."

Scarlotta gave a half-smile, then reached into her pouch and pulled out the map. It shimmered faintly—then dimmed.

"Still won't show me the way," she muttered. "It responded to you. And your friends. But not me."

Micah tilted his head. "Maybe… maybe it knows you're not supposed to go alone."

Her jaw clenched. For a heartbeat, she looked like she might say something sharp—but instead, she stood and turned away.

"I told you to get some rest, wizard. Trust me, you'll need it. We won't delay for you at dawn."

Scene: A Warning in the Shadows

Micah stirred in his bindings, the rough rope scraping against his wrists. The fire had burned low, casting strange, shifting shadows on the trees around the small encampment. The ogres—four now, after the laughing one had wandered off into legend—lay strewn about the clearing, snoring like rocks rolling through gravel.

Scarlotta sat apart from them all, her cloak drawn around her shoulders, the map open on her lap. She hadn't slept. Couldn't.

Micah shifted again and whimpered slightly in his sleep. She looked at him.

"Useless little dreamer," she whispered to herself—but the words lacked venom.

One of the ogres, the one with the chipped tusk and the habit of kicking anything that made a noise, stirred. His beady eyes opened and locked onto Micah.

The ogre stood and lumbered over, cracking his knuckles.

"I don't like how he twitches," the ogre muttered. "Maybe I knock him still for good?"

Scarlotta's head turned slightly, her expression unreadable in the firelight.

"Touch him," she said coldly, "and I'll turn your insides into beetles."

The ogre paused mid-step. "What?"

She rose slowly, deliberately, her eyes glowing faintly.

"I said," her voice softened, dangerous as velvet over steel, "go back to sleep."

The ogre hesitated. Then, grumbling under his breath, he turned and stomped back to the far side of the clearing.

Micah hadn't woken—but he mumbled something in his sleep—something about home.

Scarlotta stood still, watching the rise and fall of his chest. She knelt beside him just briefly and reached out—then stopped.

Instead, she plucked a bit of moss from his collar and whispered under her breath, "Fool."

Then she rose and returned to her seat by the map. But her gaze lingered on him longer than she'd meant it to. Too long for someone who claimed not to care.

As the sun rose the next morning, without a word to the wizard, Scarlotta freed Micah from his bindings.

"Are you letting me go?" the little wizard said hopefully.

With a withering look, Scarlotta shook her head. "Try to escape, and you will spend the rest of the journey bent over an ogre's shoulder."

Micah shuddered with revulsion and nodded vigorously to Scarlotta, his expression one of angelic innocence, and gestured shyly towards the trees while bouncing from foot to foot.

Scarlotta watched the wizard wander off toward the trees, tripping over a root and apologizing to it as if it were royalty.

"Terribly sorry, Your Rootiness."

She rolled her eyes but didn't stop the faint twitch of amusement at the corner of her lips.

As Micah darted off toward the edge of the clearing, narrowly avoiding another rogue tree root, Scarlotta shook her head in disbelief.

"Does he always talk that much?" she muttered aloud.

One of the ogres—who was mid-morning yawn—shrugged in a gesture that said probably. Then it scratched its backside and wandered off in search of something less confusing.

Left alone for a brief moment, Scarlotta stared at the wizard's departing back. He was still chattering to himself, gesturing with both hands as if holding an invisible conversation with a particularly argumentative squirrel.

She sighed.

She couldn't deny it: he was… persistent. And oddly endearing. The kind of man who might accidentally unleash a fireball while trying to light a candle, then apologize to the soot.

When she had taken him hostage, it was just leverage—a tool to unlock Jorg's Hold and reclaim what was rightfully hers. But now...

Her grip tightened on the edge of her cloak.

He was beginning to grow on her like moss—unexpected, scruffy, but surprisingly hard to shake off once it took root.

And he was the only one who'd ever looked at her without fear or calculation. Just awe. Just curiosity.

Just… kindness.

Stupid kindness.

From the trees came the crash of a bundle of sticks hitting the ground, followed by a yelp.

"I'm okay!" Micah called. "Only poked myself three times! That's a new record!"

She covered her mouth to suppress a laugh—and for a brief moment, her heart ached.

I'm not supposed to laugh, she thought. *Not with him. Not anymore. Still…*

When Micah returned, arms full of mismatched sticks (and two that were actually roots), he dumped them proudly on the ground.

"Behold! Kindling, firewood, and possibly a sentient shrub I accidentally offended. It was very vocal."

Scarlotta raised a brow.

Micah grinned and gave her a half-bow. "Lady Scarlotta, master of mystery and light-threatening daggers, I formally request your assistance with making fire—unless you've got a spell for breakfast?"

She didn't answer.

She just stared at him—at the hopeful gleam in his eyes, the way he hadn't asked for anything but company—and something shifted.

She knelt beside the kindling. "I'll show you how to build a ranger's fire," she said flatly.

"Really?" he beamed. "Will it sparkle?"

"No."

"Will it whisper secrets of the woods to me?"

"No."

"…Will it at least not explode?"

"…Hopefully."

Scarlotta stood apart from the others, arms crossed, but her ears strained toward the camp.

Behind her, Micah and a lone ogre—too dim-witted to help, too oblivious to leave—were finishing a one-sided conversation.

Micah poked at the dirt with a twig. "Y'know, I don't really think she's evil."

The ogre grunted in the affirmative, or possibly indigestion.

"I mean, yeah, she kidnapped me. And waved a dagger in my face. And tied me to a stick…" He paused. "Okay, that part wasn't great."

He glanced around, voice softening.

"But… I saw something in her eyes. She's not bad. Just…" He trailed off, searching for the word. "Lonely, maybe. Or afraid to need anyone."

The ogre blinked, rapt. Or confused. Hard to say.

Micah gave a quiet laugh. "Anyway. Don't tell her I said that, yeah? She'd probably turn me into a toad. A really chatty toad."

From her shadowed vantage point, Scarlotta froze.

Her fingers clenched tightly around her sleeve.

Lonely?

That word echoed like a pebble dropped into a forgotten well.

She hadn't heard anyone speak of her with such gentle honesty in years—maybe ever. Her power had always inspired fear. Her beauty, envy. Her name, suspicion.

But Micah—Micah Miscast—had seen something else.

And somehow, that made her feel more exposed than the worst of her crimes.

She turned her face away, blinking fast. The wind was sharp, but it wasn't enough to explain the sudden prick in her eyes.

After smothering the fire, they began their journey again, with Micah skipping along the overgrown path, chattering like a bird on its third cup of coffee.

"Look at this beautiful butterfly! Oh, and what a gorgeous cloud that is—it looks like a fat duck with a crown! And that toad over there! Have you ever seen one so warty? He has more bumps than stinky back there," he giggled, pointing at one of the ogres trudging behind them.

The ogre rumbled with mild confusion. Scarlotta said nothing, walking ahead, her shoulders tense. Micah bounded forward, undeterred.

"Hey, Scarlotta, did you hear me? If not, I can cast a spell to throw my voice! Let me see... Ah-ha!" He plunged a hand into one of his many pockets, scattering lint, cookie crumbs, and what may have been a moth.

"A pinch of rabbit fur and... a bat toe—perfect!"

He whispered, "Propelitus Vocare," swirling his fingers with theatrical flair.

There was a moment of silence. Then—WHAP.

The toad he'd admired a moment earlier launched skyward like a fleshy catapult victim and smacked directly into the back of Scarlotta's head with a most undignified splut.

Everyone froze.

Even the ogres stopped mid-stride, jaws slack.

The toad, somehow unharmed, blinked serenely, now perched like a crown atop Scarlotta's head, legs splayed and clearly enjoying the view.

Scarlotta turned with agonizing slowness.

Her eyes locked on Micah.

The forest held its breath.

Micah, caught between terror and inappropriate giggles, stared back with wide eyes.

"I... I didn't mean you! I was trying to throw my voice! Not a toad! You're not a toad! I mean—you're much more beautiful—um—I—uh..."

He trailed off, his smile shriveling as she reached up, plucked the toad off her hair like a queen lifting a teacup... and then gently placed it back on the ground.

Still silent, she turned and resumed walking.

Micah tiptoed behind her, whispering to the toad as he passed, "Run. While you still can."

Micah sat by the fire, knees tucked to his chest, unusually quiet. He fiddled with a frayed thread on his robe, avoiding eye contact with the ogres, the trees, the stars—basically the entire universe.

Across from him, Stinky was roasting something unidentifiable on a stick. The smell alone could drop a charging boar.

Something nudged Micah's foot.

He looked down.

It was the toad.

Same bumpy, lopsided creature that had launched itself (with magical assistance) directly at Scarlotta's scalp. Now it blinked up at him with bulbous affection, gave a tiny, gravelly "wrrrribbit," and leapt clumsily onto his lap.

Micah stared at it.

"You... followed me?" he whispered, glancing around to see if anyone noticed. "Why would you do that? You got flung like a warty missile. I assaulted you. With magic."

The toad blinked again. Then nestled down as if this was, indeed, its intended destination.

"…Right," Micah said, awkwardly patting its head. "Loyalty through trauma. I get it. We've all been there."

He sat there a while longer, absently stroking the toad's knobby back. After a moment, he murmured, "You know, Stumpy—no, Wartimus—hmm… maybe just Toad—Toad it is. You're probably a better spell than I've cast all year."

Behind him, a figure stirred.

Scarlotta stood in the shadows, leaning against a tree.

She watched the small wizard and his toad, heard his soft, self-deprecating words. Her expression didn't change much—but the rigid line of her shoulders softened. Just barely.

The moment passed.

She melted back into the dark.

The Next Morning

The sooner we get this quest over with, the sooner we can go our own way, Scarlotta thought bitterly. She cast a sidelong glance back at Micah, still rambling on to his loyal toad like a bard without an audience. It would've been comical—if it weren't so exhausting.

By midday, they reached a bog. The path ahead dwindled to a precarious strip of firm earth clinging between the swamp's edge and the encroaching forest. It stank of rot and brine, and the buzzing of bloated insects created a constant, maddening drone.

Eventually, the trees gave way to a field of dry grass—waist-high and sun-bleached, the kind that whispered ominously when the wind stirred.

Scarlotta halted.

Her head tilted slightly. One hand went instinctively to her dagger.

"I hear something ahead," she hissed.

She whirled toward the ogres, already annoyed to see Micah attempting to strike up a conversation with a dragonfly. "Gag the wizard!"

The ogres didn't question her. Two of them moved to Micah, who barely reacted—whether from shock or the unbearable stench of his captors, no one could say. He slumped like a sack of enchanted potatoes.

Scarlotta crouched behind a gnarled fallen tree at the edge of the field, her ranger senses flaring. Rustling ahead—slow, rhythmic. Not wind. Voices, too low to make out clearly, but guttural and deliberate.

She motioned sharply.

"You, over to that side of the road," she whispered. "You—flank them from the east. Everyone else, stay alert. We don't move until I give the word."

She fought back a grin. Finally. Something to sink her blades into.

Behind her, the ogres shuffled clumsily into their positions.

Micah, still bound and gagged, blinked blearily from beneath a rough linen wrap. The toad, somehow nestled against his boot, gave a single soft ribbit—its eyes fixed unblinkingly on the waving grass.

Galdon Kaldir Sniffles

"We're coming up to a large open area," Galdon whispered, crouched low at the edge of the dry grass field. "It's only about three feet tall. Not much cover. Every step through it will rustle and snap like twigs in a fireplace, so keep it quiet."

He turned to the others. "There's no way around. To the left is a bog—you don't want to end up in that muck—and to the right, a forest too thick to squeeze through. This is the only way forward."

Kaldir let out a low grunt of displeasure.

"You'll need to crawl," Galdon added, giving the Minotaur a once-over. "You're… somewhat noticeable."

Sniffles stifled a giggle but failed miserably. His shoulders bounced with each suppressed snort.

Kaldir's eyes narrowed dangerously. "What's so funny, gnome?"

"I—uh—it's just…" Sniffles wheezed, wiping a tear. "I was imagining what Micah would say, seeing your—your majestic posterior up in the air. Tail waving like a flag. He'd probably start composing a ballad on the spot: The Wind Beneath His Rump."

The Minotaur blinked slowly, in a way that suggested extreme violence was a viable future option.

"Right, then. Probably best we all keep quiet," Sniffles added quickly, suddenly fascinated by a blade of grass.

Galdon muttered, "Enough. Let's move."

He ducked into the golden sea of dry grass, vanishing like a shadow in wheat. Sniffles followed, crouched low, nose barely skimming the tops of the brush.

Kaldir dropped to his knees with a groan and began inching forward—his immense form creating the effect of a furry ship parting a sea of dry stalks, his tail swaying unhelpfully like a metronome set to embarrassment.

Behind them, the wind shifted ominously, bending the tall grass in an unnatural ripple.

It seemed that every movement in the grass caused the loudest rustling known to nature. Kaldir, sweating buckets and crawling like a disgruntled yak, suddenly let out a muffled grunt—his left horn had plunged into the dirt, making a furrow and entangling itself in the root-knotted grass.

"I'd love to help," Sniffles whispered, examining the mess, "but that wicked wench Scarlotta took my good dagger. I've only got this rusted thing." He held up a blade so dull it looked better suited to butter than battle.

With a sigh of eternal disappointment, Galdon pulled out a small wood axe from his belt. Kaldir's pupils dilated in sheer panic.

"You're not cutting my horn off!"

"Relax," Galdon muttered. "Unless you start mooing, your horn stays intact."

It took the last of Sniffles' emergency dwarf spirits stash—pried from a sock hidden up one pant leg—to calm Kaldir long enough to let the dwarf work. Sniffles winced at the loss but admitted privately that saving a horn (and possibly his own hide) was worth it.

By now, the sun had risen, and the air inside the tall grass had turned into a humid stew of misery. The bugs, summoned by sweat and despair, descended with gusto. They buzzed, bit, and burrowed, forming a flying cloud of pure malice.

The trio attempted to endure it with the noble grace of seasoned adventurers. That lasted twelve seconds.

With simultaneous screeches, they exploded out of the grass, flailing, slapping, and stumbling toward the road like three flammable scarecrows trying to outrun a match.

As they reached the path, the air instantly changed. The bugs vanished, as if they'd hit an invisible wall.

"Wow," Sniffles gasped, wiping his brow. "It's like there's some kind of... ward?"

"Yeah. Weird," Kaldir grunted, snatching back the skin of spirits and taking a long, greedy pull.

"I think it's more likely," said a smooth, unfamiliar voice from behind, "they just can't tolerate the smell of ogres."

The trio spun around.

WE MEET AGAIN

"For the love of all that is holy!" Galdon muttered through clenched teeth as he rounded the thicket, his eyes falling on the crumpled figure lying motionless in the grass. His voice broke through the silence like a hammer on stone. "Micah!!"

Sniffles gasped, his large nose twitching furiously as panic seized him. "Please be alive!" he shouted, bolting forward, his tiny hands already fumbling through his satchel for anything remotely medicinal— or vaguely magical—that might help.

"Not so fast, gnome," came Scarlotta's voice, cold and smooth as a dagger sliding from its sheath. She stepped from the shadows like a wraith, her blade glinting as it stopped him inches from his friend.

Sniffles skidded to a halt, eyes wide. "What's wrong with him? Why isn't he awake? Micah?"

"The wizard is fine," Scarlotta replied with a dismissive flick of her wrist. "He has a... sensitivity to the cologne my ogres insist on wearing."

Micah's eyelid fluttered, then cracked open just long enough to cast Sniffles a discreet wink. The gnome slumped in relief. "Oh, thank the gods. It's just nasal overload."

"We need to talk," Scarlotta began, straightening with the weight of someone preparing for a negotiation—or a betrayal.

"We've got nothing to say to you, Jezebel," Galdon snapped, stepping forward. "You stole from us. Kidnapped our wizard. And Sniffles' best dagger, which may be the greatest injustice of them all."

Kaldir, listing slightly from the side effects of too much dwarf brew and too little breakfast, squinted at the group like a sleepy bear peering from its cave. "Did she say something about a trinket?" he mumbled.

"I did not," Scarlotta said, eyes narrowing, "but the trinket you carry... there's more to it than you know."

Galdon muttered under his breath, "Bloody wizards and their shiny baubles."

Meanwhile, Sniffles had noticed something Micah was doing. The little wizard had, with surprising stealth, wriggled his hands free of the rope and was preparing to bolt.

Sniffles jabbed Galdon in the ribs, eyes darting to Micah and then to Scarlotta. The dwarf gave the faintest nod, the glint in his eyes betraying that he had a plan. A terrible, wonderful, ridiculous plan.

Without warning, Galdon threw back his head and sang.

It was not good.

It was not in tune.

It was not even in a key known to man or beast.

But it was loud. And it was distracting.

Scarlotta flinched. The ogres groaned and clutched their ears. Birds burst from the trees. Somewhere, a frog died of shame.

And in that moment of chaos, Micah rolled to his feet with a triumphant "Ha-HA!" and promptly tripped over the toad still loyally following him, face-planting into a pile of dry moss.

Micah, face buried in moss and dignity in tatters, groaned. "Ow. My everything." He blinked up through tufts of greenery and caught a glimpse of the chaos: Galdon howling like a banshee in mid-seizure, Sniffles pointing dramatically at nothing in particular, and Scarlotta frozen, her sword half-raised and clearly questioning her life choices.

The ogres, massive fists clamped to their heads, began to stumble in confusion.

Micah scrambled to his knees, fumbling through his pouches with the panic of someone searching for a sandwich in a burning house. "C'mon, c'mon… dried mushroom, crushed pearl, bat wing—ugh, that's not a wing, that's a toenail."

His hand closed around something. A pinch of powdered moonstone. A single glitter beetle scale. And—he hoped—a tuft of unicorn tail (or maybe horse... hard to say).

He shoved the ingredients together and thrust his hands into the air. "Flashius Glitterus Maximus!"

There was a beat of silence. Then—

BOOM!

A thunderous poof erupted around him. A blinding shockwave of iridescent glitter burst forth in all directions, accompanied by a chorus of what sounded suspiciously like enchanted chimes and one inexplicably long "ta-daaaa!"

The ogres reeled backward, shrieking. They clutched their eyes, now streaming with tears as the glitter infiltrated every nook and cranny of their faces.

"Ahhh! My eyeholes!" one bellowed, spinning blindly.

"I taste colors!" another howled, flailing.

Even Scarlotta shielded her face as a spiral of sparkles whirled past her in a dazzling blur, momentarily masking everyone's position.

Micah stood, dazed and slightly singed, blinking through the cloud of shimmering chaos. "Did… did it work?"

Sniffles, jaw unhinged, nodded slowly. "Micah… that was actually useful."

Galdon, hand over his heart, whispered, "I saw a unicorn. I swear by my beard."

Kaldir, rubbing his eyes, muttered, "I've smelled prettier things than this spell. But well done."

Scarlotta lowered her sword, blinking furiously through the haze, eyes briefly locking on Micah with an unreadable expression.

He looked sheepishly at her. "Still not friends, right?"

She didn't answer.

But she didn't stab him either.

The great glitter getaway

The clearing was chaos.

Ogres stumbled like blindfolded elephants at a barn dance, swinging clubs wildly into the trees and occasionally at each other. One was busy trying to wash his eyes out with a puddle, only to realize that it was too late, in fact, a nest of angry swamp crabs.

"RUN!" shouted Galdon, grabbing Sniffles by the collar and hurling him like a furry satchel in the direction of escape.

Micah, still glowing faintly from his sparkly triumph, attempted a heroic stride forward—but promptly tripped over a root and fell face-first into a bush.

Kaldir, now somewhat sober thanks to the sensory trauma of glitter in his fur, hoisted the wizard like a sack of potatoes over one shoulder.

"Your legs are forfeit until further notice!" he bellowed, charging after the dwarf and gnome.

Scarlotta stood frozen for a heartbeat, sword still at her side. The map clutched in her fist pulsed faintly—but so did something else in her chest. Something she didn't quite recognize. She didn't give chase.

"Stinky! Move!" she barked finally, and the ogres scrambled to regroup behind her.

But the party was already gone.

They careened through the trees in a trail of broken branches and panicked gasps. The gnome dodged between trunks like a squirrel on espresso, while Galdon barked directions and curse words in equal measure.

Micah, upside down on the Minotaur's shoulder, blinked at the canopy rushing past. "Is this what flight feels like?" he asked dreamily.

"No," Kaldir huffed. "This is what fleeing feels like."

Suddenly, Twig appeared mid-air, bobbing like a phosphorescent lantern, giggling wildly as he zoomed ahead of them. "This way! This way! I found a burrow with a friendly raccoon and mildly aggressive mushrooms!"

They didn't even ask.

The companions dove into the narrow cave just as a roar echoed through the woods—ogres realizing too late that the "glitter dragon" had been a ruse.

Inside the burrow, panting and heaving, they collapsed in a pile of bruises, laughter, and indignity.

Micah lay on his back, eyes wide, arms splayed. "That was… amazing."

Sniffles peeked down at him. "Don't let it go to your head."

Twig danced above them, his light flickering gently. "You sparkled violently. I approve."

Galdon coughed glitter. "We need a plan."

Kaldir groaned. "We need a bath."

Micah grinned, dirt in his teeth, twigs in his hair.

"We need a song," he said.

Galdon looked at him. Then at the others.

And, to everyone's horror, he opened his mouth. He was tackled to the ground and decided to keep his mouth shut.

Chapter Thirty Four: Embers in the Dark

The fire was small, little more than embers in a dug-out pit beneath a rock outcrop, their chosen hiding place for the night. A narrow shelf of stone shielded them from the wind, and dense underbrush kept their firelight muted.

They were quiet.

Micah poked a stick at the flames, his usual chatter gone. Sniffles sat cross-legged beside him, darning a tear in his cloak from the ogre's club. Even Twig's glow was softer than usual, bobbing gently as if afraid to disturb the stillness.

Kaldir leaned against the rock wall, arms crossed, fur still sparkling faintly with stubborn flecks of glitter. "I don't trust her," he said suddenly, voice low. "I mean… I did. I really did. For a moment."

Galdon, polishing his axe with a cloth that looked like it used to be part of a bard's costume, gave a grunt. "It's what she wanted. Our trust. She played us well."

Sniffles looked up. "Micah didn't want to believe it. Not really."

Micah didn't speak. He just kept poking at the embers. "She looked so sad," he said after a moment. "Back in the camp, just before I cast the spell. She looked at me like… she wasn't sure anymore."

Galdon narrowed his eyes. "Doesn't matter. Sad or not, she tied you up and handed you over to ogres."

"I know. I just…" Micah trailed off. "I don't think she's bad. Just lonely."

The silence that followed was thick.

From the shadows beyond the fire, hidden behind trees heavy with moss, Scarlotta watched. She had followed them—not with her ogres, not with a plan, but with something she didn't understand gnawing in her chest.

She'd seen the wizard's goofy magic. Heard the gnome weep for his friend. Watched the dwarf risk himself, the minotaur protect. And in that moment when Micah spoke—

"I don't think she's bad. Just lonely."

—something in her cracked.

She remembered her days in the Conclave: the cold stone halls, the chains of silence, her power drained because they feared her. Her name was erased from the spellbooks. Her heart numbed. But she had never had what these fools had.

Not loyalty.

Not laughter.

Not light.

She stepped back into the woods, deeper into shadow, her jaw tight. Her grip on the trinket in her satchel tightened.

She couldn't go back to them.

Not yet.

But now she wasn't sure she wanted to keep going forward alone either.

Scene: Scarlotta, another vision

The towering cliffs of Jorg's Hold loomed above, bathed in twilight shadow. Alone, Scarlotta stood before the moss-covered gates, their once-mighty stone doors fused shut by time and ancient enchantment. Vines curled like fingers across the faded runes etched into the rock—runes that pulsed softly, awakening as her presence disturbed the air.

She stepped closer.

A low hum vibrated through the ground beneath her boots. Then, without warning, a swirl of mist erupted from the cracks in the stone. It formed a ghostly image—her younger self.

Eyes wide, the illusion of Scarlotta was clad in a ranger's cloak and a witch's pendant. Her hair, untamed by bitterness, whipped in a phantom wind.

"You don't belong here," the illusion whispered, voice echoing with innocence and fury. "You chose ambition over loyalty. Power over people."

Scarlotta staggered back. "I never chose—" she began, but the illusion cut her off.

"You would sacrifice anything. Even yourself. Even him."

The mist swirled again, shifting now to reveal Micah, smiling—then fading into ash.

Scarlotta clenched her fists. "This hold holds more than treasure. It holds answers," she growled. "You don't know what they took from me."

The gate responded with a groan, a crack of light threading across the stone like a heartbeat. But it didn't open.

Not yet.

The vision dissipated, leaving her alone in the fading light, shaken but determined. She turned from the gate and vanished into the trees.

Aren't we almost to Jorg's Hold?

The next morning, the party continued on its meandering way to Jorg's Hold, Kaldir insisting on stopping at the only tavern left between them and Jorg's Hold for more 'supplies'. They entered the village of Tinderhook shortly before dusk, with only moments left to restock at the market.

Tavern Scene: Galdon's Grand (and Dreadful) performance setting:

A cozy, firelit inn in the village of Tindlehook. Patrons fill every seat, and the scent of stew and ale clings to the air like smoke on wool.

[Interior – The Crooked Tankard Tavern – Night]

The door slammed open with the jingle of a cracked bell. Kaldir ducked under the doorframe, nearly tripping over a decorative wagon wheel bolted to the wall. Behind him scurried Sniffles and Micah, the latter still dabbing glitter from his eyebrows. Galdon followed, arms full of parcels and a sour expression brewing on his face.

They flopped into the nearest open booth like sacks of regret, and Kaldir was already waving to the barkeep.

"One pitcher of dwarf spirits, and keep 'em coming!"

The barkeep, a thick-necked man with a face like an old boot, raised an eyebrow but nodded.

Galdon dumped the supplies unceremoniously on the table and slid into the bench. "We have a problem."

"Oh no, not again," groaned Micah, slumping forward until his face met the table with a dull bonk.

Galdon continued, "We're low on coin. If we keep drinking like this, we'll be broke before dawn."

"Well, that's not going to work," Kaldir said, already slurring. "You're a bard. Sing for our supper!"

"NO!"

Micah and Sniffles spoke in unison, their faces blanched. Sniffles gripped the edge of the table as though bracing for a lightning strike.

But Galdon was already rising, smoothing his beard like a curtain call was nigh. He approached the barkeep with the theatrical flair of a man who believed in himself far more than anyone else in the room.

"My good sir," he began, gesturing with a slight bow, "I am Galdon, bard extraordinary. Permit me to perform in exchange for our board and board."

The barkeep squinted. "And if you ain't 'extraordinary'?"

"Then we shall take our leave immediately," Galdon said proudly.

"Deal," said the barkeep without missing a beat. "Stage is yours."

[Moments Later – Tavern Stage]

A hush fell over the tavern as Galdon climbed onto the small, makeshift stage. He cleared his throat dramatically, tapping his foot twice.

Micah and Sniffles peeked from under the table, dread pooling in their stomachs like a bad stew.

Then—

"· O Wind that Blows on Gnomish Toes, Let not thy fungus flee...·"

A glass shattered.

Someone coughed, choked, then whimpered softly.

Sniffles, wincing in agony: "He's using the nasal resonance again. It's worse this time."

Kaldir groaned into his mug. "I'd rather be hit by a stampede."

"· For every goat that sings a note, another moon shall pee! ·"

The baby in the corner screamed.

The bard, undeterred, spread his arms in triumph. The final verse soared like a wounded duck trying to reach the moon.

Silence followed. One woman in the back clapped once.

"...Is it over?" whispered Micah, his face pale.

The barkeep slowly rubbed a hand over his face, looking like a man who'd stared into the void. Then he sighed. "You get one room, no meals, and you owe me a new mug."

Galdon bowed deeply. "Art moves the soul."

"Yeah," muttered a patron, "...straight outta the tavern."

[Later – Back at Their Table]

Kaldir drained what was left of the second pitcher and burped loudly. "I've fought ogres less destructive than that song."

Micah tilted his head. "I think I've forgotten my own name just to survive."

Sniffles, still under the table, whispered, "...He rhymed 'spleen' with 'latrine.'"

Galdon rejoined them with pride beaming from every pore. "That, friends, is how legends begin."

"You've started something," Kaldir muttered, "I just hope it's not an angry mob."

The crooked tankard – later that night

The stairs groaned under the weight of one surly Minotaur, a humming gnome, a whimpering wizard, and a triumphant bard.

"Here we are," Galdon said with a flourish, stopping at a crooked door labeled 'ROOM.' Just Room. No number. No fancy sign. Just a nailed-on plank with confidence.

Kaldir squinted. "This looks... small."

"It'll be fine," Galdon replied, unlocking the door with a rusty key.

The door creaked open.

There was a long silence.

It was... indeed a room. Technically. The bed was a narrow cot with one broken leg, leaning like it had seen some things. A straw-stuffed pillow sat like a defeated pancake. There was a stool missing a leg, a single candle on a cracked plate, and an ominously stained curtain that definitely hadn't been washed since the reign of the previous king.

Micah stepped in first, hopeful. "Well, at least it's—OW!"

He'd tripped over the chamber pot.

"Watch it," muttered Sniffles, crawling in after him. "That thing's armed and dangerous."

Kaldir stopped at the door and shook his head. "No way. I'm not sleeping in there with you three squeakers. I'll take the stable."

"There's no stable," Galdon said. "Just a goat tied to a cart out front."

"I'll spoon the goat before I cram into this matchbox."

"But we're a team," Micah insisted. "We share things. Food. Glory. Space. Lice."

Sniffles made a strangled noise in the corner.

"Well, someone's gotta take the bed," Galdon said, already placing his bag on it.

"Not a chance!" barked Kaldir. "Your lullaby back there was punishment enough."

"Fine," Galdon muttered, dragging his bag under the bed like a sulking dog.

Micah claimed the stool. It tipped immediately, tossing him into the curtain, which came down with a whoosh, revealing a crude painting of a duck with suspicious eyes.

Sniffles curled into the corner, nestling into the pillow. "Soft," he murmured, then added, "...sort of."

Kaldir poked his head in one last time, holding a handful of hay and a goat. "I'll be outside if anyone gets murdered. I want plausible deniability."

Micah settled at the foot of the bed like a house cat, his head resting on Galdon's boot.

"Goodnight," he mumbled. "I call first bath tomorrow."

"There's no bath," came Kaldir's voice through the wall.

A beat.

"...I call the least wet puddle," Micah corrected.

The candle flickered, casting dancing shadows on the cracked ceiling.

And for just a moment, the four of them—even Kaldir outside spooning a goat—slept in peace.

Sort of.

Morning at The Crooked Tankard

The cock crowed.

Then croaked.

Then fell silent—likely due to the exhausted, vaguely threatening groan that followed from within the tavern's lone guest room.

Inside, it looked as if a drunken whirlwind had passed through. The curtain remained in a crumpled heap. Micah's staff was stuck between the floorboards. Sniffles' arm dangled from the straw cot like a limp noodle, clinging to the pillow as though it owed him money. Galdon slept facedown with a sock on his head, mumbling rhymes in his sleep. And outside, Kaldir slowly sat up in a hay bale, his horns tangled in the goat's tether.

The Minotaur blinked, bleary-eyed. The goat bleated in sympathy.

The crooked tankard – moments later

"Get up," Galdon groaned into the mattress. "We've got a mountain to find. And possibly our dignity."

"I left mine two towns ago," Sniffles mumbled, clutching a half-eaten apple.

Micah yawned and stretched. "I dreamt I was a great and powerful wizard. Townsfolk cheered. Dragons cowered. My spells worked." He sighed. "Woke up, of course, mid-sneeze with my foot in the chamber pot again."

"That explains the smell," muttered Galdon.

Front of the Inn – Morning Fog Lifting

Their packs slung over tired shoulders and rations reduced to three bruised apples and what Micah swore was a magical cheese (it wasn't), the group reconvened in front of the inn. Kaldir rejoined them, brushing hay off his shoulders and sniffing his arm suspiciously.

"I don't think goats are meant to cuddle," he muttered.

Micah grinned. "You've got a bit of hay in your—" He reached up and tugged, and a small tuft popped from Kaldir's horn. "Ah. There we go. Majestic once more."

Sniffles pulled out the tattered map and held it up to the light. "We follow the north road until the Wyrd Tree," he said, tracing with a stubby finger. "Then cut east until the foothills. If we hurry, we can camp beneath the Jorg's Watch bluff by nightfall."

Galdon adjusted his lute, squinting at the road ahead. "Do we expect trouble today?"

"Trouble," Kaldir rumbled, "expects us."

"Right!" Micah declared, staff in hand. "Adventure awaits! Destiny calls! Also, breakfast would've been nice, but I'll settle for dramatic flair."

Sniffles rolled his eyes. "Let's just try not to trip into doom before lunch."

With boots thudding, hooves stomping, and one hopeful wizard bouncing along like a squirrel with a spellbook, the unlikely fellowship turned north, toward the next leg of their journey—and whatever waited beneath the looming shadow of Jorg's Hold.

Midday Misery and Melodrama

The road was long, the sun high, and the tempers of four mismatched companions were quickly fraying like Micah's robe hem.

"I'm telling you," Sniffles groaned, rubbing his temples as though massaging the bad decisions out of his skull, "we've got to start pacing ourselves. If I lose another brain cell, I'll start rhyming when I think."

"It's the minotaur," Micah replied, not even attempting subtlety. "He's the instigator. Spirits, brawls, midnight goat serenades—he's like chaos with horns."

Kaldir's ears twitched.

He turned slowly, eyes smoldering. The ground trembled a little as he stomped ahead, muttering darkly about "soft-footed whiners" and "the next gnome I punt into the sun."

Sniffles and Micah shared a glance. Then, as if fate itself had a sense of irony, the rock they'd been kicking idly went rogue, ricocheted off a stray root, and bonked Kaldir squarely on the back of the head.

He whirled around, fury blazing.

Each gnome and wizard immediately pointed at the other.

"HE DID IT."

Kaldir stared between the two with the slow-burning anger of a volcano re-evaluating its career choices.

Behind them, Galdon let out a hearty snort of laughter, which quickly transformed into a cough when the Minotaur shot him a look that could flay paint.

Bored of the silence that followed, Galdon raised his chin and burst into song.

Or tried to.

To say it was melodious would be to lie on the level of enchanted court jesters trying to sell ogre perfume. It screeched, it warbled, and somewhere, three squirrels fell from a tree, stunned.

Birds took to the skies. Mice stampeded. An unfortunate rabbit dove headfirst into a hollow log and refused to come out.

Kaldir grunted and, with mechanical precision, handed out small blobs of hardened tree sap—shoved into ears like nature's own mercy.

Micah blinked. "Wow. That's shockingly effective."

Sniffles nodded sagely. "I haven't heard a thing since the screech. Bliss."

Now thoroughly annoyed by the loss of potential lunch and their ungrateful reaction to his art, Galdon threw his arms up. "FINE! I will find something to eat, you bunch of tone-deaf ingrates!"

He stomped into the brush, tunelessly humming under his breath, birds scattering once more in every direction.

Micah leaned close to Sniffles. "If he comes back with a pinecone and says it's soup, I'm faking an allergy."

Sniffles nodded. "If he comes back singing again, I'm faking death."

He inched forward slowly, each creak of the branch sounding like a snide comment from the universe. "Just a little farther," he muttered, balancing like a bard on a tightrope—which, admittedly, he once tried during a tavern bet and lost two teeth.

At last, with a triumphant grin, he reached the berries. They were plump and glistening in the dappled light, practically glowing with "I-told-you-so" energy. He plucked a handful, then another, stuffing them gleefully into his pockets and—just to prove a point—into his mouth.

"Victory," he declared with a juicy smirk.

That's when he felt it.

A prickling sensation—eyes on the back of his neck. Galdon turned his head slowly, the leaves rustling like whispered warnings, and came face-to-face with a squirrel. Not just any squirrel. This one had rage in its eyes. Tiny claws clutched the branch, and it twitched its tail like a duelist preparing for a slap.

Galdon blinked. "Alright, fella, I didn't know these were your berries. I'll just—"

The squirrel let out a battle squeak and launched.

It was a blur of fluff and fury. Galdon flailed, swatting wildly, trying not to fall and not to scream—he failed at both. As the squirrel latched onto his face like a furry grappling hook, he shrieked, lost his balance, and plummeted from the tree, bouncing off each limb on the way down like a cursed pinball.

He landed with a thud, a flurry of leaves and half-eaten berries cascading around him. Silence. Then a soft plop as the squirrel dropped beside him, stood up, crossed its tiny arms, and—Galdon swore it— smirked before darting off into the underbrush.

MOMENTS LATER

Sniffles darted ahead through the underbrush, with Micah close behind, his staff bouncing rhythmically against his back.

Micah (panting):

"I hope it's not a banshee. I haven't studied anti-banshee spells yet. Closest I've got is one that repels slightly sour cheese."

Sniffles (over his shoulder):

"Better bring it just in case. Galdon might have summoned a dairy demon."

They rounded a cluster of ferns and skidded to a halt at the foot of a massive tree.

Sniffles:

"Oh no…"

Galdon lay in a tangled heap of limbs, leaves, and dented pride. His tunic was snagged in six places. His beard bristled with twigs. One eye was swollen, and the other glared defiantly at the heavens.

Galdon (groaning):

"Tree... won."

Micah (wide-eyed):

"You fought a tree?! That's advanced druid-level combat!"

Sniffles (bending down):

"Forget the tree—did it have backup?"

(He holds up a small paw print on Galdon's cheek)

"Squirrel. Definitely squirrel. Possibly elite."

Galdon (muffled):

"It had fangs the size of paring knives…"

As Sniffles helped Galdon up, Micah tried brushing off debris—but inadvertently knocked a berry into the dwarf's nose.

Micah:

"Oh! Free snack!"

Galdon (grabbing his arm):

"You so much as eat one of those berries and I'll stuff you in a tree hole till autumn."

Sniffles (cheerfully):

"Well, on the bright side... we have berries for lunch!"

He pulled out a makeshift bowl from his pack and began collecting the fruit from Galdon's crumpled pockets, whistling a happy tune.

Micah (to Galdon):

"Just think—when we tell this story later, you fought the squirrel. And won."

Galdon:

"...The squirrel laughed at me."

Micah:

"That part we leave out."

Ext. Forest trail – later that day

The group had gathered near a small patch of shade, catching their breath. Galdon stomped up, red-faced and berry-stained.

Galdon (grimly):

"I found some berries."

Kaldir (shuffling awkwardly):

"Well, uhmm… while you were gone…"

(he avoided Galdon's gaze, studying a nearby tree with great intensity)

"…we caught a rabbit."

Sniffles (muttering):

"'Caught' is a generous term. It was lying stunned between two rocks, holding its ears."

Micah (snorting):

"More like surrendering to death-by-giggle fits."

Galdon:

"Great. Where is it?"

They all exchanged sheepish glances.

Micah (carefully):

"It was a small rabbit."

Galdon (voice rising):

"I nearly died in an airborne rodent ambush, and you ate all the meat?"

Silence.

Galdon (throwing up his hands):

"Whatever. I'll eat the blasted berries."

He stalked behind them, pulling the sad handful from his pocket. The once-glorious fruit was now squashed flat, with generous helpings of lint, twigs, and something that looked suspiciously like a beetle leg.

But pride is greater than appetite.

He took a defiant bite.

Instant regret.

His eyes watered. His face twitched. The flavor was a full-body insult. But with the determination of a seasoned bard, he chewed it all.

Micah (drifting back beside him):

"Want me to dab some dwarf spirits on your nose? You said it was an angry squirrel?"

Galdon (glaring):

"He came at me like a wind-up demon. No mercy. I still hear his war cry."

Micah, trying to maintain composure, nodded solemnly.

Then paused.

Micah (wrinkling his nose):

"What is that smell? It's like… burnt cabbage mixed with guilt."

Galdon (voice strained, face reddening):

"There was… something wrong with the berries. I think… I may have had a minor incident."

Sniffles (cheerfully):

"That's fine. We'll just walk upwind until the stream."

Kaldir (dryly):

"That might be three days away."

Shortly after the berry incident

Galdon (muttering, crimson-faced):

"The map says there's a stream up ahead... I should go clean up from my, uh, tumble in the forest."

He didn't wait for a response. With the rigid gait of a man walking on stilts and the panicked pinch of dignity barely hanging on, he tottered ahead—each step a silent prayer that no further embarrassment would leak forth.

Unfortunately, it was abundantly clear from the suspiciously damp, brown-streaked patch on his trousers that the berry betrayal had claimed its final victory.

Micah (gasping, nose pinched):

"By the gods, what is that smell? Did something crawl into his britches and die screaming?"

He collapsed into a heap of wheezing laughter, then sprang up, scampering up the trail.

Micah (calling back):

"Everyone upwind! Now! For your own safety and the safety of your nostrils!"

Sniffles (snorting):

"Aye! I vote we declare the next mile a no-bard zone!"

Kaldir (grumbling but quick to follow):

"If this smell lingers, I'm shaving his beard in his sleep."

Galdon's face had gone from beet red to something closer to beetroot stew. His pride hung from his shoulders like his ruined dignity—and both sagged equally under the burden of public shame.

The path to the stream took longer than anticipated. Galdon disappeared twice into the underbrush with the haunted urgency of a man fleeing both his companions and gastrointestinal betrayal.

As Galdon squatted at the riverbank, grimacing at the indignity of laundering his dignity, Kaldir leaned on a boulder and muttered, "We should've brought a priest. For the gitchies, not you."

"I'll have you know these gitchies survived a cave-in, three bar brawls, and one particularly enthusiastic goat," Galdon replied, giving them a ceremonious swirl in the water like a flag of shame.

Micah was standing a good twenty feet away with his robes tucked under his chin, nose wrinkled. "They need their own quarantine zone," he mumbled. "A gitchie graveyard."

Sniffles was halfway between gagging and laughing, nervously chewing the edge of a dried mushroom. "Please don't wring them. I don't want to see whatever comes out."

But Galdon, determined to reclaim some measure of dignity, held them high with a dwarven flourish and flapped them in the air to dry. The wind, sensing its moment, swooped in like a trickster spirit.

Whoosh!

The undergarments soared with impossible grace, riding the breeze like a flag of dwarven defeat—smack!—right into Micah's face.

For a moment, silence.

Then a high-pitched shriek. "NOOOOOOOO!"

Micah flailed, spinning in circles with the gitchies plastered to his face like a particularly stubborn jellyfish. The others collapsed with laughter—deep, belly-wrenching guffaws that peeled layers of tension like bark from a dead tree.

Even Galdon, grumbling, had to chuckle. "Maybe the goat had the right idea."

Micah stood frozen, the soggy undergarments slowly peeling off his face like a reluctant jellyfish. The wizard's arms flailed as he shrieked, "I've been assaulted by dwarven dignity!"

Sniffles collapsed into a fit of giggles, hiccupping with each breath, while Kaldir rolled onto his side, wheezing, "By the horns of my ancestors, I needed that!"

Even Galdon couldn't help but snort, though he tried to maintain the shreds of his tattered dignity. "Consider it a gift," he muttered, wringing out the remnants of shame in the river.

Micah, recovering his composure (if not his pride), plopped down beside them. "At least we're laughing again," he said with a weak smile. "It's been too long since we just laughed."

The moment stretched, unexpectedly soft. Sniffles wiped at a tear—not from laughter this time—and said, "Yeah... let's not wait so long next time."

Kaldir nodded, solemn now. "Tomorrow, we may face curses, monsters, or worse… but today, we had flying gitchies."

Twig popped out of Micah's sleeve at that moment, glowing faintly, and performed a tiny loop in the air—like a glowing exclamation point to the absurdity of it all.

Ext. Forest clearing – nightfall

The campfire crackled, casting flickering shadows over the mismatched band of adventurers. The flames danced in Micah's eyes as he carefully rotated a stick bearing a slightly burnt rabbit leg. Kaldir lounged back against a fallen log, sharpening his axe with deliberate strokes. Sniffles sat cross-legged, meticulously cleaning his boots while humming off-key.

Galdon sat slightly apart from the others, now clean, wrapped in a blanket with a mug of lukewarm broth. His cheeks still bore a faint pink tinge, but his pride had been mostly patched back together.

A hush lingered—a rare silence between friends too tired to quarrel, too full to complain.

Micah (grinning, raising his cup):

"Ahem… I'd like to propose a toast!"

Kaldir (groaning):

"This better not involve enchanted toads again."

Micah (ignoring him):

"To Galdon. May his aim with berries someday be as sharp as his wit."

Sniffles snorted into his cup. Kaldir rumbled a low chuckle.

Sniffles (muttering):

"And may no squirrel ever cross him again."

Galdon (dryly, raising his own cup):

"May none of you ever need your underpants burned in a fire to purify your dignity."

The group burst into laughter. Even Galdon couldn't help but grin, his eyes softening.

The firelight glinted off Twig, who had nestled on a stump nearby. The sprite's tiny glow brightened faintly, a little pulse of warmth and comfort that seemed to mirror the mood of the group.

Micah leaned back and sighed contentedly.

Micah (quietly):

"You know… this whole adventuring thing—it's not just about treasure or relics. It's about this. Us. Here. Around a fire. In the middle of nowhere. Somehow surviving."

No one responded immediately. But they didn't need to.

In the darkness beyond the firelight, the trees loomed tall and ominous, but inside the circle of flames, the group finally felt… safe.

Even Galdon.

Ext. Forest edge – night – later

The fire behind him crackled softly. The others had drifted into sleep or close enough—Kaldir snoring into his elbow, Micah mumbling spells in his dreams, and Sniffles curled up with one boot still half on.

Galdon sat on a log just outside the camp's circle of light, cradling his dented mug and gazing into the woods. His nose was still a little red. So was his pride.

A soft glimmer blinked at the corner of his vision. Twig fluttered down beside him, settling lightly on a branch. His leaf-like wings folded delicately behind his back.

Twig (quietly):

"That song you sang back there… in the Valley. It wasn't just noise."

Galdon frowned, not turning to look at him.

Galdon:

"Oh no? It cleared the field of birds. And, possibly, my dignity."

Twig (serious now):

"No. I mean, it resonated. With the stones. With the land. With… me."

Galdon glanced over now. Twig glowed faintly, a soft gold light in the dark.

Twig (continuing):

"I didn't know why I stayed dim all these years. Sprites like me—we're tied to old places. Old magic. But it fades when no one remembers the songs. Or sings them. Until someone did."

There was a long pause. Galdon blinked.

Galdon:

"You're saying… I woke something?"

Twig (nodding):

"I think… You were meant to."

Galdon looked back into the dark woods, heart heavier than it had been a moment before. His fingers itched for his lute.

Galdon (quiet):

"My mother used to sing it. I didn't know what it meant. Just… always remembered the words."

Twig:

"The land remembered too."

Twig's glow brightened, casting soft light on Galdon's face—gentle and warm.

Twig (smiling):

"There's more to you than tumbleweeds and tavern tricks, Galdon. I think maybe your song isn't just part of your past—it's part of the key."

Galdon sat in silence, staring at the stars overhead. For once, he didn't crack a joke or try to shrug it off. He just… listened.

And Twig stayed by him.

Scarlotta watched from the tree line, far enough to remain unseen, close enough to hear the echoing laughter of those bumbling fools. The Minotaur's snort-chortles, the gnome's high-pitched wheezing, and even the dwarf's reluctant chuckles blended into a kind of music she hadn't heard in… gods, how long?

Her eyes narrowed against the fading light, the crimson sky casting a copper sheen over the ridiculous scene: the wizard spinning wildly, screaming with dwarven undergarments glued to his face like some cursed carnival mask.

A sound slipped from her lips before she realized—short, sharp, involuntary.

A laugh.

It caught in her throat. Her hand flew to her mouth. Where had that come from?

She leaned against a tree, letting her forehead rest against the bark. The laughter continued in the clearing, loud and free and maddeningly innocent. It clawed at something deep inside her. A memory flickered—

A fire. A girl. Her, but younger. Laughing until she cried as her brother pulled a prank on their mentor. Magic that danced for fun, not for power. A time before the Conclave. Before the vault. Before the silence.

She straightened, the amusement already evaporating like mist in sunlight, leaving behind only the hollow ache of absence.

"Fools," she murmured bitterly, but it lacked venom. Watching them, she wasn't so sure anymore who the real fool was.

RAPIDS

Kaldir, still roaring about the choppy river….."If only you could yell us over," Sniffles muttered.

Micah snorted, "What if we could?" His eyes sparkled with that all-too-familiar look of impending magical mischief.

"Don't you dare—" Galdon warned, just as Micah dug into one of his many overstuffed pockets.

"What if I cast a Bridgeus Appearium spell?" Micah asked, puffing his chest. "It's theoretical, sure, and technically illegal in three provinces, but I think—"

"No," said Kaldir.

"Definitely not," said Sniffles.

"I'm warming up to it," said Galdon, thoughtfully rubbing his still slightly singed nose.

Micah beamed. "Great! I'll need a pinch of moss, a stone shaped like a frown, and… oh! A spoon touched by moonlight." He looked up. "Which of you touched a spoon under the moon?"

Everyone stared.

"Right," Micah said, shrugging. "Wing it is."

As Micah began whispering to his staff, Kaldir backed up, tail stiff as a board. "If you conjure so much as a drop, I will leave you. I mean it."

Suddenly, Twig fluttered out of nowhere, glowing softly and singing a delicate tune. His voice, sweet and strangely harmonic, danced along the river's surface. Where his notes landed, the rapids briefly slowed, calming the whitecaps into still patches. The group stared in awe.

"Twig," Galdon whispered, "You can do that?"

Twig landed on Kaldir's horn, glowing brighter now. "Only in desperate moments of great need and theatrical tension," he said with a wink.

Too late, Micah had finished his spell....

Scarlotta had already made it across the raging river. Just upstream, around a couple of curves in the terrain, there was a bridge. *I am having the time of my life watching these fools bumble along. It's amazing that they even know their own names,* she thought to herself.

Wow, no wonder the minotaur was banned from his village. Probably for being a witless drunkard! I'm sure the Gnome had to be the village idiot and just got lost. Probably bumped into Captain, I know a spell by accident on the road. The dwarf, I am not too sure about. He is the most serious of them all. He bears watching. I might as well settle in for the show, I am sure it won't disappoint!

She grinned to herself as she got comfortable, took a swig of spirits, and prepared for her entertainment.

There was silence for a moment, then a multitude of creaking and cracking noises. Trees started falling like flies around them. The companions were dodging and screaming for dear life. Kaldir picked up the wizard just as the largest tree fell, right where he was standing. Miraculously, it ended up landing across the river, making a somewhat precarious bridge. They stood staring open-mouthed at it.

The wizard cleared his throat, managing to extricate himself from the minotaur's grasp. "I think it was a witch's hair and an ogre toenail," he said sheepishly. Behind them, they heard an angry chittering. Glancing back, they saw several angry little squirrels shaking their tiny fists at them. Before they knew it, the dwarf, looking on in horror, lurched across the tree, going so fast his feet barely touched the bark, the rest following in short order. Kaldir, running precariously across the downed tree, happened to glance up through a less dense area of trees and was sure he had seen a bridge crossing upstream. He decided now was not the time to mention that. They didn't stop until they were sure there were no deranged squirrels following them. Flopping down in exhaustion, the unlikely foursome looked at each other incredulously.

Finally, with the most serious look on his face, Kaldir asked, "Was that your squirrel's extended family?" Galdon looked at him speechless. There was the faintest chortle from behind, but it quickly erupted into the biggest belly laugh of all time. It soon became contagious, and they were all laughing at themselves for being terrified of tiny little squirrels. Jorg's mountain loomed just in the distance above them, and the sun was just setting on the horizon.

Micah was furiously writing in his spell book, journaling the "successful spell".

"Ogre Toenail and Witch Hair equals Treefall… add warning: high squirrel risk," Micah scribbled, tongue poking from the corner of his mouth.

Scarlotta, perched silently above the bridge, shook her head with half a smirk. "Fools…" she murmured—but the corner of her lip betrayed something dangerously close to fondness.

"I think we should camp here and travel the rest of the way in the morning." They found a nice mound of velvety leaves, large enough for them all to curl up in, and were soon fast asleep.

Kaldir was woken by the thief violently thrashing around. "For the love of all that is holy, what are you doing?" He asked in exasperation. "Stop it!" as he absently scratched his cheek.

"I can't, I'm so itchy I want to peel my skin off!" Shrieked Sniffles. Kaldir grabbed a branch and lit it with the still-smoldering embers of the campfire. The thief had raised red splotches on every part of his exposed skin! He noticed he had been scratching more and more as well.

The dwarf stumbled out of the woods, frantically scratching his privates with his pants around his ankles, and the wizard was rubbing his butt up against the bark of a tree! "What is going on?" the minotaur roared, as he desperately tried to reach the middle of his back with a stick.

"Well, I took some leaves to wipe my um… backside after relieving myself," Micah explained. "Then, I started to itch terribly."

"I had to pee, but I think I may have gotten too close to the leaves," the dwarf said with embarrassment.

"We all slept on them," the thief exclaimed, furiously scratching his face.

"Oh, great, how do we get rid of it?" growled the minotaur.

"I think we can make a poultice out of some tree sap and mud, which should help with the itch and soothe the inflammation. It will have to wait until morning, we don't want to stumble around in the dark and catch something else! Try to get some sleep, NOT there!!"

Morning Mischief and Mud Baths

The first rays of morning light revealed a truly tragic tableau: four miserable figures, red as boiled lobsters, sprawled in various stages of scratching, twitching, and whimpering.

Kaldir groaned as he attempted to rise but ended up falling face-first into a patch of damp earth. "Someone—please—find me a tree that bleeds healing sap or just kill me."

Sniffles, who had tied socks over his hands in a vain attempt to prevent more scratching, was humming a nonsense tune to distract himself. "This must be what betrayal by nature feels like."

Micah, still half-asleep and rubbing a muddy clump of leaves into his forehead, muttered, "Maybe... we're just allergic to destiny."

Galdon stomped over with a fistful of sap-dripping bark. "No more whining, you feeble excuses for adventurers. Sit down. We're making poultices and reclaiming our dignity."

"You gave up your dignity three itchy hours ago when you tried to bathe in squirrel pee," Sniffles shot back.

Galdon's eyebrow twitched violently. "It was dew! I thought it was dew."

As they smeared the cooling paste over their rashes, Kaldir let out a grateful sigh. "I never thought I'd say this... but thank the ancestors for tree goop."

Micah perked up, eyes glittering with mischief. "Tree goop... that sounds like a fantastic name for our adventuring company!"

"No," said everyone at once.

They sat in silence for a beat—scratched, sticky, ridiculous—but undeniably bound together. Jorg's Hold loomed ahead, but in that moment, the itch of camaraderie was just a bit stronger.

The Whispering Stones

By midmorning, the rash was mostly under control—though Galdon still refused to make eye contact with a certain mossy log he'd confused for a latrine in the night.

The group, itchy but intact, resumed its march up the narrowing path toward Jorg's Hold. The mountain loomed closer, its jagged cliffs jutting like broken teeth into the mist-wreathed sky. Gone were the jokes and jabs—replaced now by a silence broken only by the crunch of boots and hooves on gravel.

Twig fluttered beside them, unusually quiet, his normally glowing wings now a soft, flickering blue.

"We're close," he whispered, his usual chirp replaced with reverence. "Can't you feel it?"

Sniffles stopped mid-step. "Feel what?"

A breeze rolled down from the cliffs—icy despite the sun—carrying with it a sound that made them all stop.

Whispers.

Faint at first, like wind brushing reeds. But unmistakable.

Micah leaned in toward the stone path beneath them. "It's coming from the ground..."

All eyes dropped to the path—and there they saw them:

Stone markers, worn with age, rise like crooked teeth from the earth. Dozens. Hundreds. Each was etched with symbols they couldn't read. Faintly glowing. Faintly breathing.

As the group moved forward, the whispers grew louder—not words, but emotions. Regret. Grief. Desperation.

Kaldir's usual grumble faltered. He reached out to touch one of the stones... and it pulsed faintly beneath his fingers.

Twig hovered higher now, his wings casting light that illuminated faint trails carved into the rock. "These are the voices of Jorg's Hold," he said softly. "They remember everyone who fell. They remember who opened the gate... and who never returned."

"I-I feel like I've been here before," Galdon muttered, his voice hollow. "In a song... or maybe a dream."

And then Galdon—on instinct—sang. Just a single line. A fragile thread of melody in a world of ghosts.

And the stones answered.

Light traced from marker to marker, flickering like fireflies dancing in a pattern only the mountain could remember. And then—a path revealed itself. Not marked by any trail, but by that glowing light.

Twig's body flared brighter, his glow stabilizing for the first time since entering the cursed valley.

"I think... this is the way in," he said.

The party stood in stunned silence—until Micah, with genuine wonder, whispered, "I think the mountain is waiting for us."

Sniffles looked around. "Either that or it's going to eat us."

The dwarf stepped forward, voice steady. "Either way... we find out together."

The Cursed Outhouse

Along the glowing path, just past the thicket of Screaming Pines, nestled behind a mossy boulder and a faded sign that read in suspiciously cheerful script:

"Public Convenience. Definitely Not Cursed. Probably."

"That's not ominous at all," Sniffles muttered, narrowing his eyes. "I don't trust anything with that many adjectives."

Micah was hopping from foot to foot like a caffeinated rabbit. "I don't care if it's cursed, hexed, or home to an interdimensional flatulence demon—I have to go."

"It's unusually clean," Galdon said, sniffing the air. "Like... suspiciously lemon-scented."

Kaldir gave it a long, flat look. "Places like this are always cursed. Or worse. Public."

Micah didn't wait for a consensus. He dove in, slammed the door, and from inside came a brief silence.

Then: whoosh, pop, BWAHHH, and what sounded like a choir of confused chickens yodeling in reverse.

The door banged open.

Micah stumbled out backwards, glowing faintly purple, hair standing completely on end like he'd licked a lightning bolt, and trailing what appeared to be enchanted glitter fog.

"I think... the toilet talked to me," he said breathlessly. "And possibly offered me a quest?"

"You're levitating," Sniffles observed dryly, watching him hover a full inch off the ground.

"Am I cursed?!"

"No," said Galdon, eyes wide. "You're divinely exfoliated."

A rainbow briefly shimmered across Micah's skin. He sneezed and released a tiny puff of glitter from his left ear.

Kaldir walked up, kicked the outhouse door open like he expected it to attack, and squinted inside. He immediately took three slow steps back and muttered, "It's... a pocket dimension. Lined with velvet. Smells like lavender, regret, and cinnamon buns."

There was a pause.

"Was there... music?" Galdon asked.

"Yes," said Micah, haunted. "And a very judgmental towel rack."

Sniffles took notes. "Definitely adding this to the memoir. Chapter title: 'The Day the Toilet Chose a Champion.'"

Kaldir nodded once. "We burn it."

"No objections," said Micah.

They set it ablaze. It screamed. Only a little.

Then, politely rang a bell before disappearing into a swirl of smoke and sparkles.

They stood in silence.

Micah turned to the group, still gently hovering.

"I'm not touching anything magical for the rest of the day."

"That's optimistic," Sniffles said.

Let's continue and hope we dont run into anything cursed the rest of the way.

The Gates of Jorg's Hold

The path of glowing stones led them up a steep incline, twisting between gnarled trees that looked like they had been burned from the inside out. As they climbed higher, the sky darkened—not from clouds, but from shadow. The kind that felt older than night.

And then, they saw it.

Jorg's Hold.

Carved into the face of the mountain itself, the stone gateway rose like a monument to lost hope. Cracked columns framed the entrance, each one etched with fading runes and battle scars. A massive door— twice the height of Kaldir—stood sealed, its surface split down the middle like a book waiting to be opened.

But it was no ordinary door.

It pulsed with a soft, reddish light—like breathing stone. Like it knew they had come.

The group stopped at the threshold.

Micah stepped forward, gazing at the ancient door with wide eyes. "Is it... alive?"

Twig hovered in front of the door, wings humming softly. "Not alive. Remembering. These doors have not opened in a hundred years."

Galdon stepped up beside him and ran a hand across the stone. It was warm.

"I've seen something like this... once," he whispered. "Beneath the Iron Vaults. It responded to the song."

Kaldir groaned. "Not more singing. We're trying to get in, not cause an avalanche."

Micah elbowed him. "I believe in you, Galdon. Just try not to hit the squirrel note."

Sniffles ducked behind a rock. "I'm not getting launched again."

Galdon closed his eyes.

A hum escaped his throat—low at first, then rising in pitch. Not the bard's usual flamboyant performance, but something ancient. Solemn.

A bard's song to memory.

The moment the note left his lips, the runes on the door ignited— red, then gold, then blinding white.

The mountain seemed to exhale.

RUMMMMMMMMMMMBLE.

With a grinding groan that shook dust from the cliffs, the doors began to part, stone sliding against stone, revealing a black chasm beyond. Cold air spilled out, thick with the scent of time and secrets.

Inside was nothing but darkness... until Twig fluttered forward.

The little sprite hovered near the threshold—and for the first time, his glow intensified, casting golden rays that licked the walls inside the corridor as if the hold itself recognized him.

His voice was quiet, but sure. "It remembers me."

The party exchanged glances.

Micah, hand tight on his staff.

Sniffles, checking his pockets nervously.

Kaldir, swallowing hard and muttering, "Not turning back now."

Galdon, gaze steady, hand resting near his lute.

And then they stepped inside.

Meanwhile…

Scarlotta waited until the last boot disappeared down the steps.

She had followed them quietly, never close enough to be seen. And now, the door was closing.

"Not today," she hissed, and with a running start, launched herself at the narrowing crack.

She slammed shoulder-first into the gap just as the stone began to seal. One foot caught, and she had to wriggle, twist, and shove her way through with the grace of a raccoon sneaking into a pantry.

There was a dramatic scraping sound, a squawk that might've been her, and a final pop as she vanished inside.

The stone door sealed shut with a deep, echoing boom.

Silence returned to the forest.

And the party had no idea they were no longer alone.

The doors creaked shut behind them with a final, echoing BOOM.

The descent into Jorg's Hold

The entrance to Jorg's Hold loomed like the gaping maw of some forgotten beast, carved directly into the mountainside. Ivy curled down its flanks, and the air that poured from within was unnaturally cold— stale, yet laced with a whisper of long-forgotten fire.

Galdon stepped forward first, torch held high. "Well," he muttered, forcing levity, "home sweet ancestral crypt."

As they descended the crumbling stone steps, the light from outside dwindled. The torch's flame danced against the rough-hewn walls, illuminating strange carvings—some worn with time, others seemingly fresh.

The path led them into a vast chamber of pillars and shadow. And then... the air changed.

A low hum, like a distant harp string plucked, vibrated through the stone.

Suddenly, the walls flickered.

Micah froze.

Across the far end of the hall, a dozen versions of himself stood in a row—each one twisted by failure. One dropped a book, and the flames engulfed a classroom. Another sobbed over a broken wand. A third sat imprisoned in a tiny cell. The line of failures continued into the dark.

"No," he whimpered. "No—I didn't mean to—" His hand gripped his staff as if it might vanish. "I was trying to help…"

Sniffles, eyes wide, spun toward the sound of distant laughter—high-pitched, childish, familiar. Through the stone, a door flickered into view: his old village.

But it was wrong. The colors were too pale. The shadows were too long.

A tiny version of himself stared back at him from the other side of the illusion—mocked, blamed for every theft, every broken thing.

"You'll never be more than a joke," the child whispered, before fading into the stone.

Kaldir staggered as a voice echoed—one he hadn't heard in years.

"You failed the rite. A coward in the river. No place for you in the horned brotherhood." His reflection rippled across every shiny surface in the room—dripping wet, shivering, eyes wide with shame. "Weak."

He slammed a fist into a pillar—but it passed through. Just an illusion. But it still hurt.

Galdon, torch quivering, turned slowly in place. A single note, pure and crystalline, echoed through the air.

An old dwarven lullaby.

His mother's voice.

Then came the image: a hall of dwarves watching him sing—mocking, laughing, pointing at his off-key voice. The torchlight flickered. A stone at his feet cracked, revealing a tiny harp beneath, buried long ago.

"I only wanted… to be heard," he murmured.

The song lingered—and then faded.

And in that silence, a soft golden light pulsed behind them.

Twig.

The tiny sprite hovered above the ground, his light pushing the illusions back like a warm dawn. "Don't believe them," he whispered. "They're only echoes. But echoes cut deep, don't they?"

He floated to Micah and gently touched the wizard's hand. The staff glowed faintly.

To Sniffles, he offered a small acorn—carved with a laughing face.

To Kaldir, a drop of water floated to his brow, glistening like a jewel. "You're not afraid. Not anymore."

To Galdon, Twig simply said, "Sing again. But for you this time."

The spell of the hall loosened, and the companions stood—shaken, but together.

From far within the Hold, a deep tremor echoed through the stone, as if the mountain itself acknowledged their passage.

"Keep your eyes and ears open," Kaldir instructed firmly, stepping ahead with his axe resting on his shoulder.

Micah and Sniffles, ever the literal duo, immediately widened their eyes until they bulged like boiled eggs and tugged their ears forward with exaggerated concentration.

Kaldir halted mid-step and blinked back at them. "I swear by the Forge Fathers, if the mountain doesn't kill me, the embarrassment will," he muttered under his breath, then trudged on behind Galdon.

The bard, never one to suffer in silence, was softly singing a tune meant to quiet their steps—something his grandmother used to croon about tiptoeing past sleeping dragons. But his tone had slipped into something closer to a wheezing goat trying opera, and with a sudden rumble above them, a small cascade of pebbles and grit poured down from the ceiling.

Everyone froze.

Micah let out a tiny squeak.

"Nice lullaby, bard," Kaldir whispered through clenched teeth. "Woke the mountain right up."

"Too many soprano notes," Galdon admitted sheepishly, looking up at the rocks as though they'd personally betrayed him.

Regaining their nerve, they moved deeper into the tunnel. It was here that Micah decided to be helpful—he whispered an incantation and thrust his wand forward. The spell of illumination worked all too well. A blinding white light exploded from the wand's tip, illuminating the entire cavern like a sunrise in a coal mine.

The sudden flare lit Micah's ears on fire—quite literally.

"My ears! My ears are ascending to wizard heaven!" he screamed.

Sniffles hurled himself at Micah like a gnome-shaped fire blanket, pulling a soot-stained handkerchief from his sleeve and slapping it against the scorched tips with alarming dedication.

Kaldir, gritting his teeth so hard his molars ached, inhaled deeply—and caught the unmistakable stench of roasted ear. "By all the ancestors… it smells like burnt bacon in here."

"Could be worse," Sniffles said brightly. "He could have combusted something useful."

"I'm still smoldering!" Micah whined.

They pressed on. According to the map—which had now taken on an almost divine importance in their eyes—the passage would split. And when it did, they were to take the right fork and hug the wall.

Easy.

Until the wailing started.

It began as a distant moan—like a weeping wind curling through dead trees—but soon crescendoed into something raw, human, and wrong. The kind of cry that claws at your chest, trying to rip your courage free.

Micah's knees knocked together like clattering dice. Sniffles, brave in the face of most things, was now balancing on Kaldir's tail, using it like a lifeline.

"I don't like this place," Sniffles whispered.

"Congratulations," Galdon replied. "You're the last one to figure that out."

With unanimous dread, they chose the right-hand path.

Micah, cowed by the consequences of magical bravado, kept his wand tucked safely in his sleeve. Instead, he placed one hand on the wall, using it as a guide. The rock was cold and slick with condensation. At one point, it twitched.

"THE WALL MOVED," Micah hissed.

"It did not move," Kaldir replied, patting the bard's shoulder hard enough to nearly flatten him.

"Why is the ceiling breathing?" Sniffles whispered.

"It's not," Kaldir said again.

A long pause.

"…You don't sound convinced," the gnome whispered.

Their steps echoed along the right-hand corridor as the wailing behind them faded to a low sob—and the silence ahead grew louder. Something was waiting for them. But what, none could say.

And for now, that was almost worse than knowing.

"What is this treasure, anyway?" Kaldir asked casually.

The question echoed down the tunnel like a shout in a tomb.

The others jumped, their nerves already frayed thin by the oppressive silence that surrounded them. All movement ceased. They held their breath, listening—straining—for any shift in the air, any footstep, any growl in the dark.

Nothing.

They all exhaled at once.

"It doesn't really say for sure," Galdon muttered. "Could be gold. Could be diamonds. It could be a cursed tea kettle for all we know. Probably a fool's errand."

"Gold and diamonds?" Micah's eyes lit up like lanterns. "We'll be rich!"

He bounced on his heels in giddy excitement, then promptly tripped over his own enthusiasm, catching his toe in a hairline crack in the stone floor. With a yelp, he flailed and fell—landing awkwardly on a mottled, discolored stone.

Click.

The sound was subtle, but unmistakable. A low, grinding rumble followed, rising from deep beneath the stone.

"Uh-oh," whispered Sniffles.

A moment later, a second sound emerged—like a whisper turning into a roar. A distant, echoing rush.

"Is that… water?" Galdon asked, his voice tight.

It was.

And it was getting louder.

They all turned to look back—just in time to see a glimmer of liquid light flicker down the far end of the corridor.

"Oh no," Kaldir said flatly.

"Oh yes!" Micah shrieked. "RUN!"

The party broke into a sprint, boots scraping stone, lungs pumping like bellows. The roar behind them grew deafening. Cold, rushing water surged through the tunnel like a furious beast unleashed from its chains.

"This is not what treasure hunts are supposed to feel like!" Sniffles wailed, clutching his oversized pack as it bounced behind him.

"Why is it always water?" Kaldir shouted. "Why never pillows or clouds?!"

The floor beneath them trembled. The walls wept with condensation. A curve loomed ahead.

"Turn! Turn now!" Galdon barked, as they skidded around the corner—seconds ahead of the flash flood that howled behind them like a pack of angry river spirits.

"Wait—where's the dwarf?!" Sniffles shrieked, eyes wide as saucers.

The rushing water thundered past, but amidst the spray and chaos, they spotted a glint of steel—Galdon's helm—miraculously hooked on a jagged rock near the edge. His bearded face appeared beneath it, gritting his teeth as he clung to the helm like a barnacle.

"Hang on!" Kaldir bellowed, scrambling forward. He dropped to one knee and leaned dangerously over the slick edge. "Grab my horn!"

Galdon didn't hesitate. With a grunt and a desperate reach, he latched onto the Minotaur's thick, curved horn, and Kaldir yanked him up with one powerful pull, planting him safely back on dry stone.

The dwarf flopped to the ground, coughing and gasping. "That—" he wheezed, "was too close for comfort."

"What took you so long?" he huffed, water streaming from his beard like a broken fountain.

"Better late than never!" Micah said proudly, arms akimbo, beaming like he'd personally rescued him with magic and a ribbon.

Galdon gave him a look that suggested there would be vengeance. But for now, he just groaned.

"Right," Kaldir muttered, scanning the hallway. "That rock was no accident. There are traps here—more of them, I'd wager. We can't afford to keep bumbling into them."

He turned to the thief.

"Sniffles—you're up. You're the best we've got for spotting these things."

Sniffles looked like he'd just been asked to kiss a dragon.

"M-me? But—I don't—what if I miss one and we all—"

Micah leaned down, placed a hand on his shoulder, and gave him an encouraging wink. "You got this."

Sniffles looked up, eyes round and uncertain—but then he nodded. A shaky, terrified, possibly regretful nod. But a nod nonetheless.

"Okay," he squeaked. "I guess I'll just... tiptoe toward death then."

Sniffles stood at the mouth of the narrow hallway, peering into the dimness beyond. The walls were damp and close, the air thick with the musty scent of ancient stone and mildew. Shadows twisted where the torchlight dared not linger, and every echo felt like a whisper from something just out of sight.

"Right, so… just me, then?" he asked, his voice a dry squeak.

Kaldir gave him a hearty shove. "After you, O brave scout of shadows."

Muttering something unkind about "horned hypocrites," Sniffles crept forward. His gnarled hands hovered inches from the floor and walls, feeling for telltale grooves or imperfections. Every few steps, he'd drop to his belly and examine a loose tile or press gently against a section of stone with the tip of his dagger.

Micah, watching intently, leaned toward Galdon. "He's like a little ferret. A noble, slightly sweaty ferret."

Sniffles paused, turning his head. "I heard that."

He took another cautious step and immediately froze. "Wait… don't move."

Before anyone could ask why, he tapped a seemingly innocuous floor tile with his dagger. There was a loud click—and with a mechanical groan, a massive stone block slammed down from the ceiling just behind him, narrowly missing Micah's nose.

Micah let out a wheeze. "I just aged five years."

"That's what you get for insulting a noble ferret," Sniffles quipped, wiping his brow. "Alright, stay close and only walk where I walk. And if you value your limbs, no skipping."

As they inched down the corridor, the traps became increasingly elaborate—pivoting floor plates, dart-shooting walls, even a swinging axe that nearly parted Kaldir's tail from the rest of him. Sniffles danced through them with growing confidence, his instincts taking over. For once, the gnome wasn't bumbling or fumbling. He was shining.

Even Galdon had to admit, "Not bad, thief. Not bad at all."

Sniffles beamed… until he tripped over his own feet and landed snout-first into the final pressure plate at the end of the corridor.

The floor rumbled. A hidden panel groaned open.

"Well," he sniffled, rubbing his nose, "at least it wasn't a pit full of spikes this time."

SCARLOTTA

The chamber beyond the archway loomed like the hollow heart of the mountain itself—vast, echoing, and carved with ancient runes that pulsed faintly in the shadows. The air was thick with the metallic scent of old magic, as if the very stones remembered spells long since cast and secrets too heavy to die.

Scarlotta crouched low, her breath slowing as she crept into the room. Her boots scraped softly on the smooth stone floor, each step echoing farther than she liked. The room was empty—at least at first glance—but the energy was palpable, as if the walls held their breath in her presence.

Her eyes scanned the space. Faint outlines of murals flanked the chamber walls, faded with time and veiled by centuries of dust. In the center of the room stood a circular dais with a jagged pedestal—broken, but humming with dormant power.

Curious, she approached.

As she neared the pedestal, the room seemed to react. A single rune—shaped like an eye—lit up on the far wall with a subtle blue glow. She turned toward it instinctively. The pedestal pulsed, like a heartbeat waking after a long sleep.

And then—without warning—her vision fractured.

The chamber around her dimmed, blurred, and was replaced by a memory not her own. She stood—no, someone stood—on that very dais long ago. Cloaked in shadows, cloaked in power. The Conclave gathered around. Accusing. Terrified. Banishing her—Scarlotta?—no, her ancestor?

She gasped and stumbled back. The vision snapped away.

Breathing heavily, she stared at the pedestal.

"This place remembers me," she said aloud, more to the darkness than herself. "Or… who I was meant to be."

Suddenly aware she may not be alone, she scanned the shadows. The echo she had heard earlier—was it her imagination?

No. Someone—or something—was moving nearby.

She backed into the far corner of the room, hiding behind one of the rune-etched columns. If the others had come this way, they would surely pass through here.

And she needed time. Time to think. To understand why the runes remembered her. Why her magic—stripped away years ago—was flickering back to life in this cursed mountain.

The Chasm. They stood at the edge of a jaw-dropping chasm—its depths lost in swirling mist, its breadth crossed only by a treacherously narrow bridge made of fraying rope and worm-eaten planks. The wind howled up from the abyss like a chorus of ghosts daring them to try their luck.

"Well, that looks... structurally optimistic," Galdon muttered, arms crossed.

"It's a death trap," Kaldir corrected, squinting down the length of the swaying contraption. "One thousand feet across, a hundred feet down, and nothing between us and a very messy legacy but a prayer and that moldy rope."

Micah, trying to look heroic, raised his staff. "Never fear! I shall cast the wings of the mighty wyrm!" he proclaimed, striking a dramatic pose.

With a puff and a fizzle, there was a pop, and a tiny purple dragon emerged—no larger than a squirrel. It hovered before Micah's nose with a bored expression and immediately began buzzing in dizzying circles around his head, chittering noisily.

Micah blinked. "That… was not what I had in mind."

Sniffles snorted. "It's cute, though. You should keep it. Call it... Puffle."

Face red, Micah sighed and stepped onto the bridge.

The boards creaked. The ropes groaned. The dragon—Puffle—kept chittering and zipping around his head like a caffeinated bee. The more Micah swatted, the more the bridge began to sway like a drunken sailor.

"Micah, no!" Sniffles yelled, gripping one of the anchor posts.

The bridge responded with a violent shudder, pitching side to side. Micah flailed. Puffle looped.

"STOP!" Kaldir bellowed, his voice booming through the canyon like a battle cry.

Micah froze mid-step.

The bridge stilled… mostly.

"The rope," Kaldir called out, his voice lower but still urgent. "It's fraying at this end. The left side is worse, but neither will last if you keep up that jig. Move. Slowly. And don't—whatever you do—swat."

Micah gulped, nodding stiffly.

"What do I do?" he squeaked, wobbling in place.

"For one thing," Galdon growled, "stop trying to murder your mosquito-lizard and get across before we have to scrape you off a rock."

"I think it's a dragon," Micah whispered.

"Then name it Regret and get moving," Kaldir snarled.

With exaggerated care, Micah shuffled forward, step by agonizing step, Puffle now perched smugly on his shoulder. Each plank groaned under his boots, but slowly, miraculously, he reached the other side. His knees gave out the second his feet hit solid ground.

"I made it…" he whispered.

Puffle sneezed a tiny spark into his hair. "Ow!"

Behind him, Sniffles whispered to Galdon, "I don't know what's more dangerous: the chasm or Micah's magic."

"Pray we never have to choose," the dwarf grunted.

Galdon's eyes flicked toward the left rope. Fibers snapped one by one, as if counted down by fate. "Pick up the pace, dwarf," he muttered to himself, legs working double-time now.

Behind him, Kaldir stood stone-still, one hoof planted just off the support beam, watching his friends with a kind of grim resolve only warriors knew—knowing full well the rope might go before the dwarf reached the other side.

The rope groaned.

Snap.

Everyone froze. A single strand whipped away like a spider's thread caught in the wind.

"Galdon, RUN!" Micah shrieked, his purple dragon zipping about like a spark off a campfire.

Galdon ran.

Sniffles darted forward, reaching out both hands as the bridge gave one last violent lurch. The dwarf leapt—and Sniffles caught him by the wrists, falling backward with the momentum, dragging the bard over the edge just as the left rope gave way entirely.

The bridge sagged violently, now dangling by the right-side rope alone.

Kaldir stared.

He had to cross that.

"Now or never," he whispered to himself. He stepped forward—slow, deliberate, the boards beneath his hooves moaning their protest. The rope creaked, screamed…

But it held.

Each step was agony. Not from fear—though there was plenty of that—but because every fiber of the fraying rope mirrored the fear in his gut.

He was halfway.

Snap.

The whole left side of the bridge started leaning to the left, and the rope had snapped. Kaldir tried to pick up his pace, but he was running at full throttle. Suddenly, it was like he had started a free fall; his companions were screaming in terror and pointing. *Oh, no, the other side has gone, too. No amount of scrambling will get me there in time,* he thought to himself in resignation.

I just hope it is a quick death, I don't want to end up mangled at the bottom looking like Sniffles behind.

Scarlotta had caught up to the companions just before they reached the rickety bridge. "Well, that's just great. If they wreck that bridge, I will never catch up to them."

Taking the last few feet with a leap, he crashed onto the other side. Looking back, he saw the most horrendous sight imaginable. A demon with bloodshot eyes so wide they seemed to take up most of its face, and ruby red hair sticking out every which way possible, its maw stretched so wide he could see its dripping fangs, was lurching across the now teetering bridge. Shuddering in revulsion, he prayed that the bridge would collapse before the monster reached the end.

Micah was awestruck. A vision straight from the heavens was running toward him, with flaming red locks bursting free as her cap flew from her head. She was leaping with the grace of a gazelle running through the grasses of its homeland. "Come to me, my love!" He put his arms out… She dropped like a rock with a blood-curdling scream. "What just happened?" Micah asked with confusion.

"Thank goodness," Kaldir sighed in relief. "It didn't make it to this side."

"What in blazes are you blathering about? That was Scarlotta!" Micah cried with anguish. "Erm, no way," Kaldir shook his head. "Are you buffoons going to leave me hanging here all day?"

They rushed to the edge and, with trepidation, slowly looked over, afraid of what they might find. "Don't just gawk down at me! Pull me up, you bunch of morons!" Scarlotta had grabbed the frail bridge as it had let go. She unfortunately smacked into the side of the chasm on mid-swing, going down. Fortunately, she was able to get turned just enough so that her backpack took most of the blow. Kaldir and Galdon each grabbed a side and easily pulled Scarlotta up from the deep cavern.

The fire crackled to life with a pop of sap, sending embers spiraling lazily into the vaulting ceiling above them. Shadows danced on the walls of the rock wall behind them, and the air was ripe with the smell of the scorched pine that they carried with them and the sweet smell of dwarf spirits that were generously being handed around after their latest close call.

Scarlotta stretched languidly as if she hadn't nearly plummeted to her death just moments earlier. She leaned back against a rock, one leg crossed elegantly over the other, and gave Kaldir a slow, appraising smile as he nursed his skin of spirits like it was a newborn lamb.

"I must say," she purred, "Minotaurs do make excellent rescuers. Brave. Strong. Heroic." She let the last word linger like perfume.

Kaldir cleared his throat, visibly puffing out his chest as he muttered, "It's just a bit of rope. Nothing to get in a tangle over."

Across the fire, Micah beamed with misplaced pride. "Of course, of course! We all have our talents. Kaldir's is strength, Galdon's is singing."

"No, it isn't," Galdon interjected flatly, cutting into a chunk of hard cheese with a dagger that had seen better days.

"—and mine is…well, mine is leadership and magical inspiration," Micah finished, gesturing grandly with his spoon. He nearly flung half the soup into Sniffles' face.

Sniffles, brushing mystery stew from his lap, leaned over and whispered, "She's up to something. Just look at her."

"I am," Micah whispered back dreamily. "Isn't she glorious?"

"No, not that look! The scheming look. She's playing nice—but only because she has another trick coming."

Micah frowned, his brow furrowing for a whole three seconds before smoothing back into a dazed smile as Scarlotta laughed at something Kaldir said.

Galdon glanced around the fire and shifted uncomfortably. He stared into the flames, jaw tight, until he finally muttered, "You didn't answer my question, Scarlotta. What are you doing here?"

She tilted her head, as if considering whether to lie or deflect. Finally, she gave a half-smile. "I had a…change of heart."

"Really?" Galdon's voice dripped with skepticism. "Funny, I've heard ogres make better apologies."

"I didn't come to apologize," she replied coolly, taking a sip from her skin. "I came because there's something in Jorg's Hold I need. And whether I like it or not," her eyes flicked across the group, lingering on Micah for a moment longer than necessary, "you lot are the key."

Sniffles puffed up. "You betrayed us. Tied up Micah, knocked us all out, stole our map!"

She sighed, swirling the spirit in her skin. "And if I recall, you picked my pocket and tried to poison me with your atrocious cooking."

"Touché," Micah said, raising his spoon in salute.

"Enough!" Galdon barked. "You're not fooling me with smiles and spirits. Try anything—anything—and I swear by the beard of Morgran, I'll hurl you into the next trap we find."

"Duly noted," she said sweetly, clearly unfazed. "Now drink up, boys. We'll need our strength for what's coming."

Micah leaned back and sighed dreamily. "She called me boy."

Sniffles covered his face with both hands.

As night deepened, the fire's warmth wrapped around them, an uneasy peace settling like mist. Galdon sat with one eye open, still gripping his dagger. Kaldir dozed beside Scarlotta, already snoring gently. Sniffles kept mumbling defensive scenarios in his sleep.

And Scarlotta… sat still, watching the flames with a wistfulness she couldn't explain—her fingers idly tracing the edges of the half-map she kept tucked beneath her cloak.

As the five companions dozed around the flickering campfire — the smoke curling like ghostly fingers into the air of Jorg's Hold — a low hum began to thrum in the very stones beneath them, disturbing them with its insistent rumble. At first, they thought it was the wind groaning through the tunnels. But the fire, once yellow and warm, flickered abruptly to a cold blue hue, and they all sat up with alarm.

Micah looked immediately at his plate of leftover roasted mushrooms (which he'd failed to fully cook, as usual), wondering if they were still fit to eat, and furrowed his brow. "Did someone cast something? Because if not… I think something's casting us."

"I feel that too," Scarlotta said quietly, her hand subtly reaching toward her dagger — not out of threat, but instinct. Even Galdon stopped mid-swig of dwarf spirits, his eyes narrowing as he scanned the shadows.

The moment all five locked eyes across the fire, the humming grew louder, like a resonating chord struck beneath the earth. Then, from the wall behind them, a faded mural carved in the stone — one none of them had noticed before — began to glow faintly.

Twinkling light licked the edges of the ancient relief, revealing a scene of five figures: a horned beast, a red-haired enchantress, a small figure with a hooked nose, a minstrel holding a strange instrument, and a robed spellcaster holding a burning orb.

"That looks… like us," Sniffles breathed.

"No, no, no. That's just a coincidence," Kaldir muttered, though his voice lacked conviction.

As the glow intensified, the air rippled with ancient magic. The mural pulsed once — a beat like a heart — and then, as if on cue, the stones behind it shifted. Grinding and scraping echoed through the chamber as a hidden archway unfurled in slow motion, like a yawning mouth awakening after centuries of silence.

A gust of air burst forth from the opening, bringing with it the scent of damp moss, rusted metal… and something more elusive — memory.

Each of them heard something in that wind:

- Scarlotta heard the whispers of her mother's voice, long forgotten, calling her name from beyond the veil.
- Micah heard an old teacher's gentle encouragement… from a time before he botched his first spell.
- Galdon swore he heard the first song he ever sang — the one his mother hummed while braiding his beard as a child.

- Sniffles heard laughter — not mockery, but real, joyful laughter. His village, before everything changed.
- And Kaldir, he heard the toll of the war horn that summoned him away from home… and the single bell that rang when he didn't return.

"What in all the realms is this?" Galdon asked, voice low and reverent.

"It's… responding to us," Scarlotta said. "To all of us. Together."

Micah pointed at the newly revealed corridor. "Guys… it wants us to go in."

Kaldir groaned. "Let me guess — the one place we don't want to go is the only place we now must go?"

Scarlotta stood, brushing soot from her cloak. "We're no longer just stumbling through this. Jorg's Hold has seen us — and it's waking up."

And with that, they gathered their packs, stood shoulder to shoulder — and stepped into the breathing dark.

Scene: The Echoing Antechamber of Jorg's Hold

The last ember of their campfire crackled softly in the chamber behind them, and a flush of warmth enveloped them, but it wasn't just the warmth that clung to them from the fire; it was a pulse, ancient and humming, rippling outward from the center of the next chamber. Without realizing what they were doing, they stood side by side in the center of the room, waiting for something. As the curiosity on their faces faded, their eyes grew heavy, and the stone beneath them vibrated subtly.

Suddenly, a faint chime rang out—like a bell submerged in water. All five of them froze.

The walls of the chamber flickered with faint, rune-like patterns—glowing briefly before disappearing again. The air changed. It was no longer just musty and old—it was aware.

Micah squinted into the darkness. "Anyone else see that?" he slurred, forcing his voice to respond and trying to focus through his half-closed eyes.

Before they could respond, a low groan echoed through the hold—followed by a grinding rumble. One of the walls, previously solid and unyielding, shifted and parted like two curtains of stone, revealing five branching paths—each marked with a sigil faintly matching a figure around the fire.

A voice—old and cracked like dried earth—whispered, "One light. One voice. One truth. One loss. One vow."

Galdon, eyes wide, touched his chest. "That song I sang in the valley… it wasn't just to wake the relic. It was to wake me."

Sniffles peered toward a path lined with broken locks and half-smashed traps. "That one's calling me," he said, gulping.

Kaldir's path flickered with torchlight and the shadow of his younger, nobler self. Micah's glimmered with arcane symbols—erratic, playful, yet full of potential.

And Scarlotta's? A swirling mist lay beyond her arch, whispering promises of power—and glimpses of who she once was.

Twig, glowing faintly now, hovered at the center. "You've each touched the valley. Now you must touch the Hold. Only then will the final gate open."

INTO THE HEART OF JORG'S HOLD

The stairs spiraled downward for what felt like hours. At first, there was light—a gentle green glow from the rune-lined walls. Then there was darkness. Then there was Galdon's singing, which was somehow worse than both.

"I'm just saying," Galdon warbled, "if we die down here, at least it'll be on beat!"

"Please stop," Sniffles said. "My ears are threatening legal action."

Kaldir grunted. "Your voice is going to wake something ugly."

Scarlotta rolled her eyes. "Too late. It's already singing."

Just as Micah was about to fake a magical emergency to silence them all, the stairs ended in a large circular stone chamber. Five archways loomed in the walls, each glowing with a different colored rune, like some ancient, cursed game show set.

A pedestal stood in the center. On it, a plaque that read:

"CHOOSE THY CHAMBER. NO BACKSIES. NO WHINING."

"...Okay," Micah said, glancing around. "That's... cheerful."

Sniffles tilted his head. "That's not a normal ancient language. That's 'ancient magical sass.'"

One by one, the arches reacted to each of them.

- Micah's glowed bright violet and emitted a faint humming noise, like a spell trying to remember lyrics.

- Sniffles' glowed gold and released a puff of sarcasm.
- Kaldir's turned solid gray and vibrated slightly, as if bracing itself.
- Galdon's glowed a musical green and emitted a short trumpet fanfare that sounded suspiciously off-key.
- Scarlotta's arch turned scarlet with a dramatic spark and a faint, magical whisper that said, "Well, well, well…"

She arched a brow. "Did my door just flirt with me?"

"Your door's got good taste," said Galdon, winking.

Micah flushed.

"Ignore them," Scarlotta said, stepping closer to her arch. "If this thing tries to judge me, I'll judge it right back."

The pedestal updated itself again with a puff of light:

"ALL PARTICIPANTS MUST ENTER THEIR DESIGNATED TRIAL CHAMBER. REFUSAL IS FUTILE. ALSO, BRING SNACKS."

Kaldir grunted. "I don't like this place."

"You don't like any place," Sniffles replied.

"I liked that tavern in Dwarf Hollow."

"You fell through the floor."

"Best nap I ever had."

Micah took a deep breath. "Alright... we go in, we survive whatever trial is in there, and we meet back here. Easy."

"Survive," Sniffles repeated. "Yes, very comforting. I definitely won't be eaten by my feelings."

"Try not to explode anything," Scarlotta said to Micah as she passed him.

Micah stammered something about feathers and destiny and tripped over the pedestal.

One by one, they stepped into their arches and disappeared.

The doors sealed shut behind them with a deep, echoing boom.

And Jorg's Hold got very, very quiet.

Micah's Chamber – "The Hall of Echoed Failures"

The passage narrows as Micah steps forward alone, torchlight flickering off damp stone. The moment his foot crosses the threshold, a ripple of magic courses through the air. The torch sputters and dies—and then re-lights in a blue glow, revealing an expansive chamber filled with mirrors. But not ordinary ones.

Each mirror holds a different version of Micah—some older, some younger, some scarred, some radiant. One is proud and powerful, draped in a sorcerer's robes with followers at his feet. Another is disheveled, sitting alone in rags. Yet they all turn to face him, their mouths moving in unison.

"Why couldn't you be me?" they whisper.

Micah steps forward, trembling. One mirror shatters as he nears, revealing a moment from his youth—a young Micah standing in front of the High Council, his spell fizzled into confetti, the judges laughing. Another mirror fractures, showing the day he accidentally set his master's beard on fire.

The room is a museum of magical mediocrity—and shame.

But then, one small mirror remains whole. In it, Micah sees himself exactly as he is now—disheveled, awkward, holding a bent wand—and smiling. It's the only one smiling back.

From behind the mirror, a small rune begins to glow. As Micah reaches out and touches it, the chamber hums. A hidden sigil burns into the ground beneath him, and a low rumble echoes through Jorg's Hold as the portal opens a little further.

Micah clutches his heart and whispers, "I'm not the best... but I'm still here."

He exits the chamber, a little taller than before.

Sniffles' Chamber – "The Village of Shadows"

Sniffles creeps into the next chamber, his nose twitching, eyes darting left and right. The moment he steps inside, the torchlight behind him extinguishes. A thick fog rises, curling around his legs and whiskers.

The stone walls melt away, and he blinks in disbelief.

He's standing in his old village—only… wrong.

The buildings are twisted, leaning at odd angles. The sky above is a sickly gray, and whispers curl on the wind. Children with hollow eyes run past him laughing—not with joy, but mockery. "There goes Sniffles the sneak! Can't even pick a pocket without crying!"

He sees himself as a child, tiny, dirt-smudged, reaching into a bread cart and getting caught. The crowd in the vision laughs, even his own family shaking their heads in shame.

He stumbles backward into another scene. This time, his childhood home. His mother weeps as guards drag a man away—his father. "He stole to feed us," she cries. "And now we've lost him too."

Sniffles lowers his head, trembling. "I was just trying to help… I never meant for it to get so bad."

Then, a sound: jingling.

From the alley behind him, his younger self appears again—but instead of stealing, he's offering a coin to a crying child.

The child vanishes in golden mist, and the coin falls into the dirt— glowing.

Sniffles picks it up. As his fingers close around it, the ground trembles softly, and the mists vanish.

A carved stone door opens behind him, revealing the group's path forward—and another portion of the portal awakens deep within Jorg's Hold.

He walks out, quiet, but with something healed in his heart.

Kaldir's Chamber – "The Horns of Honor"

Kaldir steps into a stone chamber that immediately seals shut behind him. He exhales, ears twitching warily. The room is round and echoing, lit by soft torchlight that casts long shadows on the worn carvings covering every inch of the stone walls.

They depict minotaurs—proud, regal, armored. Warriors. Leaders. One carving shows a mighty chieftain raising a battle standard high. Another shows a minotaur shielding children from a fiery blaze. All of them... noble.

Kaldir stares for a long moment, then slowly removes the skin of spirits from his belt and lets it drop to the floor with a heavy thump.

"I'm not like them," he mutters.

From the far end of the chamber, a shimmering apparition materializes—young, bright-eyed, upright, proud. It's Kaldir—but not as he is now. This one walks with dignity, no sway, no flask. His horns are polished, his gaze direct.

"You were meant to lead," the apparition says calmly.

"I failed," the real Kaldir growls. "Too many fights. Too much drink. I left before they could cast me out."

The younger Kaldir steps forward. "You fled because you feared what you were becoming. But you can still choose who you are."

The real Kaldir lowers his head. "How?"

The walls begin to glow. The carving of the chieftain pulses with golden light. The younger version places a hand on Kaldir's chest.

"Take the weight. Lead again—not through power, but through sacrifice."

A deep rumble echoes through the stone. A relic horn embedded in the wall—one that had been cracked and weathered—mends itself, glowing brightly. Kaldir steps forward and lifts it, the magic thrumming in his grip.

The door opens behind him. The portal deep within Jorg's Hold stirs once more, unfolding another piece of its riddle.

He exits the chamber quietly, the horn strapped to his back—and for once, the skin of spirits left behind.

Galdon's Chamber: The Echoing Songhall

The walls pulsed with a low hum as Galdon stepped into the chamber alone. The hallway behind him sealed shut with a whisper of finality. Before him stretched an immense stone amphitheater—abandoned, echoing, and filled with empty marble seats. Ancient carvings of dwarves in mid-song lined the walls, mouths open in a silent chorus. A single spotlight of amber light streamed down from a crevice high above, illuminating a cracked stone stage.

The moment his boots touched the stage, a spectral audience shimmered to life—ghostly dwarves cloaked in ceremonial garb, eyes glowing faintly, watching him with an unsettling stillness. At the center, directly opposite him, sat a vision of his father—stern, disappointed, and silent.

Galdon swallowed hard.

He remembered this place. Or a place like it. The Grand Hall of his youth, where he once sang to acclaim—before his voice faltered during the Rite of Binding and the audience laughed. He had fled that night. Fled his clan. Fled his shame.

Now the chamber demanded he sing again.

From the silence rose a low note. Not his. It came from deep within the chamber itself. A challenge. A call. Galdon's knees wobbled, but he clenched his fists. Then, softly at first, he began to hum.

His song started off shaky—off-key, even. But as he sang of loss, shame, and hope, his voice steadied. The magic in his music—the true power he never trusted—awoke. The walls began to shimmer with gold-threaded memories: his companions' laughter, their ridiculous misadventures, the burning shame of failure... and the raw courage to keep singing anyway.

A deep rumble echoed beneath the stage as runes flared to life beneath his feet. The spectral audience rose as one, heads bowed in reverence. Even the image of his father—just for a breath—smiled.

Then, with a thunderous hum, the amphitheater shattered into mist, and Galdon found himself alone again, back in the hallway, a new glyph glowing on the portal wall behind him.

The chambers released them one by one, the stone doors groaning open as if Jorg's Hold itself exhaled in relief.

Micah stumbled out first, eyes red-rimmed and wild with thoughts he couldn't yet speak aloud. He clutched a book bound in starlight and soot—his trial still lingering in his tremors. The tiny purple dragon fluttered loyally above his head, looping through the air like a guardian wisp.

Sniffles followed next, a bit quieter than usual, the glint in his eye tempered by a weight he hadn't carried before. The key he earned now hung on a leather cord around his neck, warm against his chest.

Kaldir emerged from the shadows soon after, his shoulders broader, posture solemn. His fur bore fresh streaks of white—earned not from age but from something ancient brushing too close. In his hand was an old crest, singed but glowing faintly with his family's forgotten honor.

Then Scarlotta.

She stepped from her chamber with narrowed eyes, every part of her on guard. Her hair was a storm cloud of curls and power, but for the first time in a long while, something soft lingered in her gaze. She said nothing, but the wind seemed to follow her now, curling protectively around her boots.

And finally, Galdon—the dwarf bard—stumbled forward, eyes glassy but bright with purpose. He held no relic, no key, only a song quietly playing from his lips. The last note echoed like a bell through the stone corridors.

The glow emanating from the doors behind them revealed another chamber, swallowed in a velvet dark lit only by torchlight flickering against damp stone in ancient iron sconces. Scarlotta, her eyes narrowed, stepped forward cautiously, her hand resting lightly on the dagger at her hip—not Sniffles' this time, but one she had hidden even from the ogres.

The others approached slowly behind her, drawn in by a mix of dread and fascination. The room was round, the ceiling domed and carved with celestial symbols. Dust and cobwebs veiled intricate runes on the walls, and at its center, an altar, cracked but still pulsing faintly with blue light.

Twig fluttered forward and landed softly on the edge of the altar. His wings shimmered brighter than before, casting dancing lights across their faces. "This place remembers," he whispered, his voice echoing with an otherworldly resonance.

Micah moved toward the altar, compelled. "I've seen this in my dreams," he murmured.

Scarlotta watched him, the soft light reflecting in her eyes. For the briefest moment, she wasn't the cold, calculating ranger—but someone caught between memory and possibility.

The runes on the wall lit up faintly. One by one.

Galdon approached with reverence, humming low and slow—the same melody the spirits had echoed in the Valley of Despair. As the song filled the chamber, the altar responded. A section of the floor trembled, and a spiral staircase slowly descended into the earth.

Twig turned to them, eyes wide. "The next trial waits below... but not all of you will come out the same."

They stood together, staring at a great stone arch carved into the cliff at the mountain's heart.

A portal, barely open, emitted a faint hum, like a heartbeat barely audible beneath the stone.

It throbbed with a deep crimson glow, then flared—a sudden blast of silver light arcing outward, forcing all five of them to stagger back. The air rippled. Runes etched across the arch lit up in sequence, each one tied to the object—or person—that had just awakened something deep within themselves.

Then, with a boom like thunder rolling across forgotten hills, the center of the portal swirled open like the eye of a storm.

The tiny dragon zipped forward instinctively, circling the portal and releasing a puff of sparkling breath that shimmered across the threshold. It turned back to Micah and chirped twice—then landed on his shoulder, as if to say, I'm going too.

The five stood silently, shoulder to shoulder.

None of them had all the answers.

But for the first time since they entered Jorg's Hold, they were ready to step forward together.

Even Scarlotta didn't flinch when Micah gently offered her his elbow. She didn't take it, of course. But she didn't refuse it either.

The wind whirled from the portal like a whisper from another world.

And they stepped through.